BODIES of WORK

CLAY MCLEOD CHAPMAN

TITAN BOOKS

Bodies of Work
Hardback edition ISBN: 9781835415931
E-book edition ISBN: 9781835415948

Published by Titan Books
A division of Titan Publishing Group Ltd
144 Southwark Street, London SE1 0UP
www.titanbooks.com

First edition: April 2026
10 9 8 7 6 5 4 3 2 1

A CIP catalogue record for this title is available from the British Library.

EU RP (for authorities only)
eucomply OÜ, Pärnu mnt. 139b-14, 11317 Tallinn, Estonia
hello@eucompliancepartner.com, +3375690241

Designed and typeset in Adobe Garamond Pro and Courier New by Richard Mason.

Printed and bound by CPI (UK) Ltd, Croydon, CR0 4YY.

"Clay McLeod Chapman's *Bodies of Work* is a scalpel, and you cannot read this book without being reshaped by it. It is a rot-crumbled tale of human brokenness, clear-eyed and visceral, awful, tragic and somehow exquisitely triumphant. But as with all of Chapman's work: it comes at a cost."

Chris Panatier, author of *The Redemption of Morgan Bright*

"Ornate and remarkably intricate for such a slender book, encountering Clay McLeod Chapman's *Bodies of Work* for the first time feels both startling and exhilarating like discovering a broken relic of long-since forgotten art. A profane hymn screaming from the charnel pit of a blood-clogged throat, an obscene portrait torn from careless, withered hands—this novella is deeply subversive, absorbing, and original."

Eric LaRocca, author of *Things Have Gotten Worse Since We Last Spoke*

"In prose both fevered and stunning, Clay McLeod Chapman takes us into the world of a tormented killer—and into the minds of the young women whose lives he steals. Colorful and haunting, *Bodies of Work* stitches together beauty and cruelty, madness and imagination, as it plays all our best feelings against each other. A compelling and brutal read that proves Chapman is a true master of horror."

Wendy N. Wagner, author of *Girl in the Creek*

"Fantasy and reality warp and blend in a pure Chapman product, where a serial killer's demented fantasies give bloom to creative carnage on the canvas of his victims' bodies. Sad, sickening, and weirdly sweet, *Bodies of Work* is an unflinching window into the horrors of one way-too-dedicated artist's demented creative process."

Bitter Karella, Hugo nominated author of *Moonflow*

Also by Clay McLeod Chapman
and available from Titan Books

WHAT KIND OF MOTHER
WAKE UP AND OPEN YOUR EYES
ACQUIRED TASTE

to H.—

"Am I a real enemy of the cross,
or a very very sorry saint?"

– Henry Darger

the sixth muse

As the unofficial archivists of Winston Kemper's art, not to mention his muses, we find ourselves in the privileged position of being the foremost scholars of his body of work.

We are, in fact, the bodies of his work.

If not us, then who?

He murdered me first, so I should be the one to start his story . . .

That's not true. I was first.

Not true, not true!

Well, I was his favorite . . .

That's a lie and you know it!

And we're to believe you? Since when did you become the trusted source on—

Sssh! Do you feel that?

Feel what?

Here comes another . . .

Already?

How long has it been? I've lost count . . .

A year, I believe?

Try ten.

Quiet! It's starting again . . .

Winston finds the sixth sister much like the rest of us, delivered unto him at church. We always arrive at Shiloh Baptist when it is our time—never early, never a moment too late—even if he feels the strain on his faith almost as much as in his own weary body.

Just as he's about to lose hope, just when he wonders if he'll never find another muse again . . .

There she is! There we *always* are.

Do our names matter?

Not to him.

Her name is Kendra Weathers. Middle name Anne, after her grandmother, not that she ever uses it. On her fourth birthday, her grandma bought her a stuffed bunny with peach-colored buttons for eyes. Professor Howdy. Kendra never went anywhere without him . . . until she accidentally left him behind at a roadside restaurant during a family trip. It took three hours for Kendra to realize her best friend wasn't sitting next to her, but by then, no amount of crying was turning their car around. Not as far as her father was concerned.

Kendra's first heartbreak. The first of many.

Join the club.

Hush.

Winston will never know this about her. Our stories never hold significance to him, there and gone. Who she is, who any of us were in this world, matters very little. To him.

It's what she will become in his mind that matters, what we all became.

Butterflies.

Kendra is Winston's muse. His sixth, at long last. The answer to his relentless prayers.

It has been much, much easier to answer his divine

calling here, at Shiloh. Far easier than at the group home. Or in the rest stop. He never fails to find inspiration amongst its aisles of hand-worn mahogany pews, much the same way Winston imagines those renaissance painters God spoke to. Michelangelo. Da Vinci.

Hadn't angels inspired them to greatness as well? Did that place Winston amongst these master craftsmen, serving his higher calling?

He uses the backroom to aid in his holy summons. For years, Winston has had the space all to himself. To scribble. Dabble, perhaps, with paint. Even clip—

snip

snip

—out pictures from the various abandoned magazines left behind by parishioners. He's been able to attend to matters much more efficiently since he's called Shiloh home.

Now they are taking all that away.

Blasted leaky ceiling. A hole has opened somewhere in the tin roof, sending rain seeping through the beams, causing extensive water damage. He'll be homeless soon.

No more studio for Winston.

He has to be far more careful now. More patient. *Watchful eyes* and all that, at his back. Always peeking. Always following him at work.

Inspiration only comes but once in a blue moon. He's had to bide his time before receiving that divine lightning bolt, the archangels delivering his next muse.

But time is running out. His own body is beginning to shrivel in on itself.

So Winston prays. Prays for her arrival.

Doesn't sound like He's listening, pal . . . Sorry.

Don't speak too soon . . .

You feel it, too? What is that?

Her.

It has been raining all evening. The storm pummels the roof, a shower of nails against Winston's skull. It sounds cataclysmic. He's heard nail guns before, the gunshot of pressurized air firing one steel bolt after another into the roofing of a random house. Now those retorts are legion, an endless rapid fire, each and every nail driving right into his skull—*sssplunk-ssssplunk!*—giving him a fresh migraine.

Until Shiloh raises enough funds to mend its panels, Winston periodically replaces the mop buckets underneath the leaks in the backroom. It is such an expansive space, used for storage, ample enough to fit a cot and a desk, along with Winston's growing collection. Nobody else goes back there unless they need a fresh roll of toilet paper.

Winston has had the space all to himself.

In his younger years, Winston would've been the one to fix the roof. No longer. He's far too old to find his way up a ladder, his knees too sore to take the strain. His bones moan under the most menial task these days, leaving him helpless to tend to his responsibilities.

The church is now bleeding. Leaking.

Winston prefers the church over his last place of residence. The group home was absolutely awful. Everyone stealing from each other. Here, Winston is in the presence of angels. He attends services morning and afternoon, sitting in the rear pew. Most families attend on Sundays. Tuesdays and Wednesdays are nearly all but empty.

Sometimes he has a service all to himself. He loves those the most. He will absorb the words, take them into his heart, as if he were an entire congregation.

Winston's capacity to love Christ for more than just himself is almost enough to make up for Shiloh's dwindling attendance.

His heart is enough, isn't it?

The rain will wreak havoc on the grounds tomorrow, he just knows it. The private cemetery out back becomes all soggy when it storms like this. Loosens the tombstones like old teeth in gray gums. No one ever visits these graves anymore. Only Winston.

In the morning, he will be sure to survey the grounds for any damage. Upright the headstones again. Make sure the steel drums are still sealed, nice and tight. No leakage. No spills. Double-check that nothing tipped over. That means getting muddy. Trudging through puddles. Getting his boots caked in red clay.

Tomorrow. Tonight, he has the church all to himself. The roar of the rain. The wrath of it is almost exciting. Listen to God sending his storm. A flood is surely going to come.

That would certainly be a sign, wouldn't it?

What if it washed Winston away?

We should be so lucky.

He will stay here, alone. Simply sit in a pew and listen to the storm against the roof. His skull. He lights a few candles around the sanctuary, saying a prayer for his butterflies.

As soon as he makes his way through the nave, walking down the center aisle of pews, he senses a density in the air. A gathering of electricity, gaining power. A presence.

Someone is here. He knows it straight away.

A new muse.

She is near. Oh, how long it has been since he's felt this! He'd almost forgot. It takes his breath away, this strain on his chest, a brick weighing down his lungs.

Winston halts. Takes in the nave. The pews, all empty.

Save for one.

There. Third row. Left aisle.

No. Please, no . . . Not another.

Stop. Make him stop.

How?

Try something . . . We have to at least try.

The wooden seat glistens. Water droplets. Rain.

Tears.

She's come because she has nowhere else to go. She had a fight with her boyfriend, her father kicked her out, her husband left, she lost her job . . . It's the same story, even if the details fluctuate. Our outfits change, our hairstyles vary, but it's always the same.

Fate put this woman on a path. That path narrowed, her options dwindling down to this very night on this very planet at this very house of worship, leading her here.

To him. Winston has been patient and his patience is now rewarded.

There she is, at long last.

Shivering wet. Already her body blurs in watercolors. The hues ripple and distort, the very atmosphere around her skin seeping—*bleeding*—in fluctuating blues and reds.

He sees her wings.

Winston makes his way down the aisle, slowly, taking his time. Holding his breath. Even then, the electricity is gathering. Collecting ions. Charging the air.

She's the one. He feels it, the very disruption of her, whoever she may be.

What else is there?

He stops before the pew and finds her, all curled up. A lost cat. She's wearing a jean jacket, still damp from the rain. It's probably a lighter shade when the denim is dry, but now it's a dark, bruised blue hue. There are rings on her fingers, so many, too many, her knuckles shine, even in the dim light, causing him to wince. Gawdy things. Awful things.

He'll take those cheap things off when the time is right,

one ring at a time. Toss them all away in the church's dumpster out back. Jewelry. Necklaces. Earrings. Bracelets. Metal of all kinds, some precious, most not. Silver. Copper. Always on their bodies, but no longer. Winston doesn't keep their jewelry. Not even the cross that woman wore around her neck.

That was mine. My aunt gave that cross to me.

No—it was mine. From my husband.

Sterling silver?

White gold.

No matter now. We no longer need trivial trinkets of love or devotion or beauty. Winston has given us all butterfly wings.

This woman has yet to see him. Her defenses are down. She thinks she is still alone.

Until . . .

Kendra turns and starts, breath catching—what a glorious sound, that gasp—kicking further back in the pew, sliding away a few inches. *Clink, clink,* her fingers go against the pew as her hand skitters across the scuffed wooden paneling.

"I'm sorry," she says. She keeps her arms wrapped around herself, shivering still. "I—I didn't know anyone was here. I called out but . . . nobody answered."

It's difficult for Winston to find his voice. He's rarely called upon to speak, so he remains stubbornly mute. Dumbly staring back at this young woman. Gawking, almost.

"I just needed a place to get out of the rain."

The rain, yes. Of course. She hears it, too, those nails pounding against his head.

Winston has never been a good gauge of someone's age. She could be twenty or thirty or somewhere in between. Younger, perhaps? He can't tell. She's older than he understands, her existence such a mystery. Women have always been a mystery to him.

You can say that again.

Hush. If you're not going to constructively contribute, you can keep quiet.

Fine.

She's twenty-seven. Homeless, though Kendra is always quick to tell folks she's between homes. A bad breakup with her last boyfriend left her living out of her car for a week or so. What's left of that piece of shit. A rusted muffler temporarily took her mobile home away and now she's royally screwed, stranded in this backwater town. It's been in the auto shop for three days, going on four now that the weekend is here and they are apparently not open on Sundays for some asinine reason, her Hyundai held hostage by the goddamn mechanic until she can fork over four hundred fucking dollars for parts and labor. That fucking thief. Kendra never has that kind of money on her, even when she was working at the A&P in Warrenton, which, let's be honest, was no way to live, so she's been looking for work, any kind of work, but not *that* kind of work, and finding very fucking little.

The church was her only choice tonight. A roof over her head during the heavy rain.

"Hope that's okay," she says with a pitiful smile, a soggy shrug of her shoulders, offering her sob story in hopes that he will take pity and let her stay. Just for tonight.

Is Winston even listening? Do the words sink in? He simply stares back, nodding at the oddest intervals, strangely out of sync with her spiel. It's almost like he's pretending to listen, acknowledging the receipt of her words without comprehending them.

It's enough to send a shiver through Kendra's spine. Maybe it's just the cold.

Maybe.

What's the worry? Just look at this old guy. He's perfectly harmless. His oyster gray eyes are so wide, whiskered jaw slack, he's practically ogling over her.

There's no way he'd send her back out there in the rain . . . Is there?

Don't worry, Kendra—we all thought the exact same thing. Letting our guard down.

You're not alone.

She'll be one of us before long.

She's not yet. Don't count your chickens.

Soon. Unless . . .

Unless?

Maybe she breaks free? Breaks the cycle?

Good luck with that.

Well, she could . . .

It's already too late. Just look at the way he's staring at her . . .

Even now she's so bright, it nearly blinds him. The colors seeping out from her skin. Her body aches to break open, let the rainbow within unfurl and flood. Spread her wings.

She's one of them. *One of us.* The sixth sister.

He found her, at long last.

This process takes years. Waiting for inspiration to strike, that divine lightning bolt to his brain. The timing always needs to be right. It couldn't be during the day. Not when others rummage about the church. It always needs to be at night, when Winston has Shiloh all to himself. When the House of God is now his. For a fleeting moment, he's the only god here.

"Tea?" It comes out of his mouth as a dehydrated croak. Such a raspy bullfrog.

The word makes no sense to her. "Sorry?"

Winston swallows. Tries again. "Would you like some tea?"

She can't help but laugh—just the slightest exhale—her shoulders relenting. *Tea*. Hot tea. Of course. "Do you have a towel? Something to dry off with?"

Oily rainbows swirl about her. She's still dripping, her hair wet with rain. It's a ruddy auburn, glistening in the candlelight, so it looks like rust dribbling down her copper locks.

She's beautiful.

We all were. Once.

Not anymore.

Says you.

You think you're still a sight for sore eyes?

Worse. If anyone laid eyes on you now . . . they'd probably shriek.

The split ends reach her shoulders, soaking her sleeves. Her face holds just the faintest trace of her childhood, her youth lost in these subsequent years of hard living.

Is that a black eye he spies? Bound to be. The last gasp of her capillaries receding into a faint yellow and green. What luscious colors. She must be running away.

We all come to Winston hurt in some way. Purple watercolors. Bruised black and blue hues. The wounds are what have drawn us here, fresh or no, compelled to escape whatever life we had before intersecting with his.

Would Winston have changed his mind if we had shared our scars with him? Told him the story behind each and every one of our bruises? It seems unlikely, even now.

The compassion he expresses is purely perfunctory. A performance; not a great one. Just enough for us to lower our guard. Our biggest mistake in a life of mistakes. So many bad choices—yet our judgment of this foolish, doddering old man may be the worst.

She is already transforming in his eyes, encasing herself

in a cocoon of watercolor, ready to emerge. A warrior with wings.

What does that make Winston?

The bard of butterflies.

The next chapter is about to begin.

Does Winston know Kendra is pregnant? Of course not. She doesn't even realize it herself, unaware of the transformation that is slowly occurring within her own body.

But we do. Just look at her. That glow.

This is a secret kept from herself, carrying it deep within, a nested doll, one forgotten woman after another, awaiting the same fate, the littlest of them all barely budding.

Winston nods, mumbles, "Towel," then turns, beckoning Kendra to follow him.

Into the backroom.

He steps to the side, gesturing for her to enter first—*After you.*

How cordial.

"So," Kendra starts as she walks past him. "Do you always work this late or is this—"

The hammer comes first. A blow to the back of Kendra's head when she least expects it.

We never expect it.

Inspiration hits. A crack at the back of the skull.

The scissors are always last. That final punctuation mark to her life story.

The end.

For now.

Time flows differently now, for us, here, now that we are . . . this. So, while Kendra is still fresh in our minds, her name on our tongues, before she fades away like the rest of us, absorbed into this liminal existence that we all share now, let us tell Kendra's story—the end of it, at least—for it is the end of all our stories.

No one has called out for Kendra in ages. The very thought of her—*Kendra*—hasn't passed through the minds of anyone for quite some time now.

Nobody is looking for her. Missing her.

The obsolescence of her existence, the finality of her fading away, feels so complete, so cruel to us, because it happened to ourselves. We were just like her. Once.

Our bodies don't belong. There is nowhere we can fit in Winston's imagination, the very excess of our corpses, our flesh, incongruous to his creative process. His technique.

Winston keeps the parts he needs—our voices—and wedges the rest.

In the aftermath of Hurricane Aubrey, there was a surplus of food donations to local churches throughout the coastal towns here in Virginia. A handful of 55-gallon steel drums found their way to Shiloh to aid in recovery efforts. Seven, to be exact. The precise number of cocoons required to complete their metamorphosis, just as God intended.

How fitting! Just the number of drums he needed. What luck!

The metal canisters remain stacked behind the church. Forgotten, mostly, by now. A bureaucratic eyesore for Shiloh to figure out at some point. Just not now. Not yet. It's been years and still nothing. FEMA won't take the barrels back, now that hurricane recovery has come and gone. So they remain, slowly eroding into the soil. Leaking their contents.

Each vat has a removable lid fastened by a bolt ring, sealed tight. Whatever food is inside—rice, likely—has been there for years. Whether it's edible or not is another concern.

Shiloh has its own dumpster in the parking lot. Every Wednesday morning at ten-thirty on the dot, like clockwork, the garbagemen arrive and dispose of whatever is inside.

That gives Winston less than seven hours. Six, if he's lucky.

Years ago, he could finish in three.

He was much younger then. Now his knees complain. His back aches. His body protests more the longer he's on his feet. He tries to push the pain to the back of his mind.

There's work to be done. Much too much work.

Winston wanders to the back of the church building. All seven barrels are stacked together, two on two, with a lone drum on its own. He starts there. Taps the drum with his shoe. It sloshes. That one's spoken for. He moves to the next, giving it a tap with his heel.

This one skitters, raindrops on tin. Grain. There's still rice inside.

Perfect.

Years back, he could empty the barrel simply by tipping it over into the dumpster. Now he needs to take a mop bucket from the janitor's closet and scoop the rice out, emptying the moldering foodstuff into the dumpster, one bucketful at a time. It's slow going, this process, but it's the best his body can offer. He needs to be careful about spillage. He's sowing the lot with rice. The trail of grains tethering the dumpster and the barrel will be a tipoff to someone, surely, so Winston puts in a prayer for the birds to come to his aid, assisting him on his mission by pecking at what he leaves behind, much like the woodland creatures helped Snow White clean her kitchen, whistling while she worked.

All of God's little creatures help Winston in his time of need.

He needs all the help he can get.

It'll be dawn before he's tucked her in. Winston needs to hurry. Church services are scheduled for eleven AM and he's hoping to attend.

To give thanks. Gratitude to God for delivering another butterfly. For sending him . . .

For sending . . . whatshername.

He never remembers, does he?

Susanne.

Tamara.

Caroline.

Rochelle.

Gail.

Whispers now, growing fainter. Our names fading along with our voices.

Ssh . . . Children should be seen, not heard.

We all had names at one point, all of them long forgotten. Winston never knew them. He may have asked, but he was never listening. Never needed to know.

We are his muses. Divine inspiration sent from heaven itself. We came to Winston in his time of need, answering his prayers, the clouds parting, sunlight heralding our arrival. The watercolors radiating all around us, our skin. Brushstrokes of God.

The flesh forgets. It fades. Decays. So do our own stories, locked in our bodies. Before long, we will all be gone. Everything that's left of us. Everything that remains.

We exist only in the pages of Winston's epic.

His magnum opus.

He took our voices. Snipped that tender church bell dangling from the roofs of our mouths with his dulled fabric shears, cumbersomely plunging the blades in and cutting what he wanted from us. The anatomy of our mouths was a bit of a mystery to him, along with everything else about our bodies. Not that it mattered. In Winston's mind, that piece of pink flesh was where our sweetness resided—our innocence—the succulence of it.

He wanted to keep a part of us. A memento from our mouths. Our voices. Our laughter. The rest may have been for God, but *this* he kept for himself.

A guilty pleasure, perhaps.

No one, not even our Winston, is without a little bit of sin. Keeping these bits of us is his, taking pride in his work. Each individual divot of clipped skin is sealed in its own four-ounce canning jar, intended for preserves. The quilted crystal and mottled embossing distorting the tender fleck bleeding at the very bottom.

Perhaps he imagines we are fireflies, the sound of us, our screaming, our pleading preserved just for him. A killing jar for our whispers, our last words now desiccated husks crusted against the inside of the jar. All his lovely butterflies.

He didn't label them and so our names never made their way onto the lids. There is no way of discerning whose uvula is whose anymore, shriveling into scabs along each jar's glass bottom. But he knew our voices so well.

Ssh. Quiet down now and listen.

Listen closely.

Can you hear us? We cry as one voice now.

Speak as one.

He can hear them, even now.

Forever.

Whenever he opens a mason jar—our homes, our prisons—he can hear us again. Those last begging gasps before the blood flooded into our mouths, drowning our final cries. He's always brought back to the moment he silenced us, reliving that slice of his shears, relishing the gag, the blood spilling over our cheeks, all over again.

Winston, we whisper unheard, trapped behind glass. *We hear you, Winston . . .*

We are the salvation you seek . . .

Set us free, Winston . . .

Set us free . . .

He never listens. The glass is too much, impenetrable. He's far too occupied with his art, anyhow. What pictures he cuts out from the catalogues, what pieces he cuts out from our mouths, it all blends together. We are a chorus of the voiceless. So many of us now.

There are so many years between us. We never met, not in this life. We never knew his other victims existed until Winston brought us all together; a sisterhood of sorts.

But we're getting ahead of ourselves. This is not our story, no matter how desperate we are to tell it. Share ourselves. Nobody wants to hear from us. The victims.

You want *him*.

Winston.

How could this happen, you ask? *How could something like this go on for so long and nobody notice? How could he get away with something so heinous, for all these years?*

Simple, we say. *Easy as pie*. Happens all the time.

Who are we? Forgotten women. Lost souls that slipped through the cracks.

No one's looking for us. No one cares. Only Winston. Maybe we were mothers at one point in our lives, now gone. Forgotten sisters. Daughters to someone, but no more.

We are Winston's nested dolls. Ghosts within ghosts. We will share his story, because what other story is there left to tell?

We are merely forgotten footnotes in a world that trotted all over us.

So, we tell his.

His name is Winston Kemper. The bard of butterflies.

Let us sing for him.

Hear us! Our story, our song! We are the forgotten women. The muses of Winston. We have transformed, transcended, metamorphosized.

We have a story to tell, a song to sing.

Do you hear it? It's starting. Something stirs beneath steel. It's faint, but there. Skin bristling against rusted metal. Dissolving in her own bodily fluids. Hatching for Winston.

Observe! Hark, the herald angels scream!

The time has come to watch the butterfly crawl out from her cocoon . . .

Here she comes! That's it! Push! Push!

Puuush!

THE BIRTH OF A BUTTERFLY:

In Which We Have The Privilege Of Witnessing A New Butterfly Girl Born... See Her Emerge From Her Rusted Cocoon... How Tuckered She Must Be!

There's no light.

No air.

Such asphyxiating conditions. She can't breathe inside here. Her shoulders press inward. Arms wrapped around her own torso, hugging herself. Her knees are pressed against her chest, legs folded into themselves, pinning her in place.

Stuffed.

She must escape before it's too late!

But what is this? When she tries to release herself, let go of her own grip around her waist, her elbows immediately meet metal, metal at all sides, up and down and all around, punctuated by a pair of tinny *thwonks* at either side.

What on earth is this awful place? What's happened to me? Where am I? The questions pick up their pace, frantic now, racing through her mind, making her dizzy. *What's going on? What is this? Where oh where am I?*

Her breathing picks up as well, the air so thin she can taste the heat of her own spent oxygen, rich with carbon dioxide, pennies at the back of her throat.

What is this what's happening where oh where am I, she can't stop herself, even now, the questions continuing to spin, spin, spin, *what is this what's happening where oh where am I what is this what's happening where oh where*...

She tilts her head back. The cradle of her cranium strikes metal. She feels the brittle flakes of rust scraping against her scalp and scattering into her hair.

So dark. No light. No air!

There is a fluid of some sort settled around her waist. She feels it now, the warmth of it, thick and viscous. What is she swimming in? It's far too gooey to be water. Some syrup, no doubt, settling at her navel, rising up higher and higher, at her chest now, clinging to her skin, sticking to the surface of this metal vessel.

She needs to break free. Escape. But how?

Thrashing now. Getting liquid everywhere. On her chin. Her belly. She can't stand to be trapped inside this metal shell for much longer. She's set to lose her mind. So she pushes. Hands against the inner rim of whatever trap this is.

A coffin, perhaps? Or cocoon?

The metal relents, beginning to give. The very rust of it has softened over time, corrosion eating away at the hull. She simply has to push harder.

Harder.

Force it open. She can feel the flakes of rust dig into the skin along her palms, biting in. Cutting her. Still, she pushes harder.

Harder.

That's it! It's folding. <u>Flexing</u>. Keep pushing!

<u>Harder!</u>

Then...

A rupture in the hull. She feels the barrier give, soft metal fissuring, until her hand forces its way through. She cuts herself on the rusted grit, tiny flecks gnawing on her forearm, but no matter. She's finally through!

Light finds her skin. She sees herself, her limbs, sticky and wet, glistening in this flaccid bath. All she needs to do now is force herself out.

The crown of her head emerges. Whole flaps of rusted metal bulge outward along with her egress, peeling back to let her through.

She gasps for fresh air the moment her head is free. She keeps her eyes closed, gummed up from the feel of it, the light too bright for her to see just yet.

She keeps pushing.

The exertion is exhausting. She's spent, but not even halfway free. A snagged fowl. Her shoulders have shimmied out, now her upper torso tapers along. The puddle of fluids helps her escape, greasing the gears as it were, allowing her to slip out from the thin fissure. She flops over, hitting soft ground.

The rest of her body—waist, then legs—slither along, no longer folded over.

She's finally free.

Free at last!

She's emerged from her rusted cocoon, freshly hatched. But the sheer exertion of it all, the energy it took to break free and crawl out... it's much too much for her. She can't remember a thing. How she got here. Her own name.

Who am I?

Her chrysalis looks much like a steel drum that has collapsed in on itself, the structural integrity of the metal long forsaken, leaving behind the hollow husk of a flattened canister. FEMA, it reads. Stenciled letters.

What on earth is a fema? A female something or other?

She has no idea.

Tired now. So tired. She'll simply lie here, on the soft ground. She'll close her eyes. Feel the cool air on her skin. The breeze on her cheeks. And breathe.

Simply breathe in the fresh air...

Her throat. Why does it hurt so? What is this soreness at the very back of her mouth that makes it so hard to swallow? To breathe?

Rest. That's all she needs. She needs to rest. Regain her energy.

Sleep now.

Sleep...

artist studio

TO RENT: a single room apartment situated directly above a two-door carport. A set of outdoor stairs lead directly to an elevated entrance along the side of the garage.

"I know it's not much," Catherine Calvert singsongs, "but it sure could be a cozy bachelor pad. My husband is desperate to turn it into his own man cave, but I absolutely refused . . ."

I don't like her.

Hush.

Well, it's true . . . So fussy.

She should know better. There's no way she'll rent the place to him . . .

Is that a bet?

You're on.

Catherine walks into the apartment first, realizing Winston has yet to follow. "It has its own kitchenette," she continues. "Walk-in shower."

Winston ducks his head before entering. Such a meek

little man. He takes in the space, his wet eyes sliding over the room. Never settling on one spot long. He mumbles under his breath, calculating.

There's no way we can live in here . . .

It's so . . . small.

Suffocating.

"There's a bed you can use," Catherine offers, pointing to the mattress resting on a metal-slatted frame, tucked off into the far corner. "Or we'd be happy to take it away, if you have your own. Whatever works best."

The view is of the driveway, a strip of blackened asphalt leading to the street. A neglected basketball hoop is bolted to the garage's façade, eclipsing the window.

"Very private," she says. "Very quiet."

Winston frowns, perhaps. Catherine can't quite tell what pickled expression he's just made under his mustache. Such an untamed thatch. A wriggling caterpillar.

Fred and Catherine Calvert made the decision to rent out the room above their garage a few months after their youngest son finally moved out for college.

This empty nest needs to be filled, Catherine said to Henry. Given life again. Things are so quiet now around their house. The second-floor attic above the carport had been the boys' play space. Their sons—Nate and Brian—never had a treehouse, even with the dense expanse of coniferous trees enclosing their home, creating a canopy of softwood.

The carport is secluded enough that the boys could steer clear of their parents' prying eyes but still be within shouting distance. In middle school, the brothers traded baseball cards here. In high school, they invited girls upstairs. Fondled and pawed. The hint of cigarettes still drifts through, the smell of exhaled smoke steeped into the woodwork.

We used to know boys like that. Fell prey to them now and again.

Speak for yourself.

A little too late to be all high and mighty now, isn't it?

Shut up.

"What was that?" Catherine asks. "I'm sorry, did you say something?"

"Nothing," Winston mumbles.

She heard us.

Sure she did.

Didn't she?

Doubtful.

Then how do you explain—

"The plumbing works just fine." Catherine turns on the faucet to prove her point, letting it run, its spigot hissing. "Lovely water pressure."

Winston peers into the bathroom, barely big enough to fit one hunched body. His shoulders slump. The shower is separate from the toilet, built directly into the wall, sectioned off by a soap-scummed shower curtain featuring a seashell and starfish pattern.

"We should probably change that," Catherine offers.

Winston remains stubbornly mute through the whole interview. Always mincing his lips under that mustache. Fretting, almost. Muttering. He rarely meets her eyes, if ever, only by accident, mumbling just under his breath, as if he is having a separate conversation with himself. What was he saying? Were those words?

She should call the police.

No, she should run.

She should shoot him right where he stands. Say he was trespassing. The police will believe her.

She doesn't know any better. She thinks he's harmless.

They all do.

We did.

"There's no stove, but a hot plate should suffice. We might even have one for you . . ."

Winston examines the walls. "A clear canvas," he marvels.

"Pardon?"

"Clean."

"We, ah, have a space heater in the house you might want to borrow. For winter."

Truth be told, Winston wasn't the first to respond to the advert Catherine placed in the paper. He's not even the most ideal tenant. But she feels for him. A pang. She takes pity on this poor old man. Just look at him. *He must be so lonely*, she thinks. *So alone.*

Not alone. He has us.

All of us.

Don't you, Winston? We'll keep you company . . .

Stop it.

What?

You're encouraging him.

Am I? What kind of encouragement do you think he needs from us? Seems to be doing just fine all by himself . . .

Winston has always been the town's own lost cause, having drifted throughout the rest of Virginia and never settling. A pilgrimage, one might say.

Brandywine is the closest thing to home. How long he's been here, exactly, he can never quite recall. Years, now. Where he had been before remains a bit of a muttered mystery. Something about a boy's school, he mentions. A stint in the military, which is a lie.

Not that Catherine could tell.

And the church! Always church. Shiloh Baptist has

been his home for so long now, right down the road, a mere twenty-minute walk from the Calverts'. A perfect commute.

Winston's references came from Shiloh—letters of recommendation from the deacon, the mission coordinator, even the youth ministry leader.

Winston still works there as a janitor. A regular ol' Mr. Fixit. Whatever needs mending, whether mowing the lawn, fixing light fixtures, repairing leaks. Winston is happy to handle it. His meager income is enough to put a roof over his head. Food on the table.

"Do you have a car?" Catherine asks.

Winston shakes his head, *no*, opening a cabinet in the kitchenette. He studies the bare shelves, before closing the door and moving on.

"You must get a lot of exercise. All that walking."

"Walking," he repeats.

People know of Winston without knowing him. He isn't so much a stranger as a texture to their small town. Catherine remembers spotting him traipsing along the road's shoulder, oblivious to traffic, lost in his thoughts. His own world. Always mumbling.

Has she ever spoken to him? Certainly she must have, at some point, but now she can't quite recall.

"This must be more space than you're used to." Catherine suddenly wonders if she should be alone with Winston, or if her husband should be present.

Finally. Took her long enough.

"Why leave?"

"Water damage." Two words. It's the most he's said at once all afternoon.

There is something so simple to Winston. One might say *off*. Harmless, really. The only person he might be capable of harming is himself. How he has survived this long, on his own, is anybody's guess. The old man can barely take care of himself.

Just look at his clothes. He has probably been wearing the same outfit for years now. A threadbare corduroy jacket, light brown, with elbow patches. Is that even his jacket? Or did it come from some Lost and Found at the church? It probably has, hasn't it? Along with everything else in his meager wardrobe. Abandoned pants and forgotten mismatched socks. No wonder his clothes don't fit his scrawny frame, all loose. His collared shirt, completely wrinkled, sags over his chest. Moth-gnawed and sapped of all its color.

Oh, no, not that dirty shirt again . . . Pick a clean one, Winston.

You want to play dress-up now?

If he'd simply listen to us for once, we could help him pick out better clothes . . .

He's not a doll. Not our toy.

Of course not. We're his.

Catherine can't help but feel the compulsion to mend his jacket. It's the mother in her. *Waste not, want not . . .* Maybe there are a few shirts left behind by her sons. She could offer them to Winston. A housewarming gift. Hand-me-downs from her boys. They might not be Winston's style—*did he even care about such things?*—but it's worth offering.

God, yes, please . . . Anything other than this mismatched Lost and Found bric-a-brac.

Who cares what he wears? I don't . . .

Catherine had spent these last few years settling her own father's affairs after a long, drawn-out battle against dementia, spending his final days in a home for senior citizens suffering from probable Alzheimer's. She had to slowly say goodbye, one visit at a time, increments of his memory slipping out from his mind, who he was, long gone now, along with the muscle memory, the ability to swallow, all of him erased before her eyes.

Perhaps that's why she takes such pity on Winston. Here's a second chance. There is something so raggedy to this man: a fraying teddy bear from her childhood, seams beginning to split, tufts of gray hair spilling from his ears. She could never bring herself to throw such a beloved stuffed animal away, holding onto it for years, even as it fell apart.

Catherine says yes before consulting with her husband. Fred had been resistant to the idea of renting out the garage apartment in the first place. He preferred to use the kids' clubhouse for storage. But no, it's her decision. She holds the purse-strings around here. This benevolent gesture is hers, all hers, helping poor Winston. Giving this old man a home.

"First and last month's rent," she says. "Two hundred dollars."

Winston only has one month.

"That'll do just fine," she says, smiling. "I trust you."

Winston frowns. Perhaps.

See? Told you so . . . I knew she'd give it to him.

Fine, fine, you win. Happy now?

At least we're out of the church . . .

Finally.

Catherine feels as if she's doing some good. Such benevolence. She'll sleep well tonight, not to mention every other night for nearly a decade with Winston only paces away from her bed, having never heard our cries. The last gasp before the scissors clipped.

That harsh gargle.

Winston Kemper lives above the Calverts' garage for the next eight quiet years.

Eight years. Gone in a gasp.

It's seven.

Eight.

Are you sure? I could've sworn it was seven . . .

Definitely eight.

You're rounding up, that's why.

Forgive me if I don't know the exact number . . .

Are you counting? Marking the days down?

I might as well be. You have another way to pass the time?

It's eight. Eight years. Gone.

Where did all that time go?

Nowhere.

Stuck here. With him. In his head. In this suffocating apartment.

Winston always keeps to himself. Never makes a peep.

An ideal tenant.

Catherine occasionally forgets the man is even here—*out of sight, out of mind*—a languid silence seeping out from the carport, so close to their home and yet miles away.

Children should be seen, not heard . . .

Winston always pays his rent on time, no matter what. Always cash, kept in a coffee can. *Chock full o' Nuts*. Back at Shiloh, the parishioners take a collection, donating money for his expenses. It's unclear if Kemper has a banking account, let alone a checkbook.

Let's keep this off the books, Catherine had said at the time, for both of their sakes. Catherine was concerned about the taxman, while Winston only had his muses in mind.

Winston always seems as though he is in his own world, which is true.

This renovated storage space, this garage attic, is all

Winston has, and it has quickly become the total expanse of his life. His home is a closed loop, tiny in its circumference. His days are spent in relative solitude, far away from everyone. Never bothering anyone or drawing attention his way. Most days, it's easy enough for the Calverts to forget he's here.

That he even exists.

Lucky them.

What I wouldn't give to forget him . . .

Then who'd be left to remember us?

Winston's imagination, however, travels far beyond the limited scale of his simple existence. Winston is a god here, in this room, lording over distant worlds well beyond the bounds of our own. He leaves his frail body behind and journeys forward into his work.

Into his stories. His pictures.

Over time, the space changes. After rummaging through dumpsters and various lost and founds, Winston cultivates a workspace to complete his masterpiece—*The Butterfly Girls: or, The Epic Tale of the Final Battle in the Nether Realm of Nevermore, the Last Siege of Sisterhood, Ending the Century of Slavery Once and For All and Liberating Every Last Boy and Girl*—along with its accompanying illustrations. His voluminous opus fills the space.

Let's look around the apartment, shall we?

You're a tour guide now?

Beats just sitting here.

Fine. Lead the way . . .

One might notice the mildewing pillars first. Towers of department store catalogues stemming back decades. Sears Roebuck. JC Penny's. Montgomery Ward.

Fall fashion. Summer trends. Daisy fresh favorites. Back-to-school bargains.

Years of curling pages piled so high, they resemble yellowing stalagmites in a cave system. The covers are frayed, having been flipped through over and over again.

Pick any catalogue—*careful, be careful, don't let the towers topple over!*—and one might find every page pecked clean of its pictures. The photos are no longer where they used to be, snipped and clipped and stored elsewhere, filed away in Winston's meticulous system. The negative space of the page remains, glossy chasms where the model had been. One can still see their outline, the contours of their body, their head, their hair, while the actual image is missing. Snipped out of this existence.

Where is that photograph now? Where did the girl in the picture go?

The walls. Look at the walls.

There are children everywhere.

Running. Laughing. Sometimes it's just their lips. Or eyes. The glossy bits and pieces, taped to the walls. Scattered across the ceiling. Flickering loosely in whatever breeze drifts in from the open window. There isn't an inch of wall space that isn't covered with children, all of them running, giggling, taken out of the context of their catalogue and repurposed in some unnerving tableau. So many distorted scenes. A collage of bodies.

You have entered an art gallery of an unwell mind.

Take a moment to focus. Let your eyes adjust.

Now you're beginning to see.

Look at the painting. *If you can even call it a painting.* Long, sprawling. It takes over all four walls. This untitled fresco suspends itself across the apartment, overwhelming the wall space, consuming it, a panoramic portrait made from watercolors, pencil, and carbon tracing paper overlaid across several sheets of butcher paper, bound together by clear packing tape to expand the parameters of the canvas.

Enormous, isn't it? Breathtaking?

He certainly took ours . . .

The curled canvas reaches the corner of the cramped space and continues on, running along the neighboring wall before meeting the edge of yet another painting.

Step up close and one might feel as if they've immersed themselves in the portrait. Absorbed by its bleeding colors.

The painting itself appears to depict a war. Which one, exactly, is difficult to say. Different wars from different eras blend together into one blackened morass of battle. There are soldiers in gas masks, wielding bayoneted rifles, trudging through muddy trenches. They intermingle with Confederate rebs, battling alongside one another, even though there are a hundred years between them, now cruel comrades in the field.

It makes absolutely no sense.

You're no art critic.

I could be, looking at his stuff . . .

Winston's work doesn't count.

Not far off is a poppy field. An odd assortment of flowers bursts out from the ground in an explosion of blurring watercolors. Blossoms of all kinds tower overhead. Even these feel off-putting. The flowers themselves are far too big, distorted in their own proportions.

A group of girls race through this field of flowers. Each child is adorned with antlers of various shapes and points, like a stampede of young women running into battle.

They have butterfly wings. Some fly, their feet lifting off from the ground, soaring through the air. It is a marvelous sight, seeing these horned girls take flight.

What are they doing in this war?

There is something so striking about their expressions. Recognizable, perhaps. It's there, *right there*, the faintest hint of familiarity, whispering at the back of your mind.

Where have you seen these faces before?

There. Suddenly it comes to you.

The Morton Salt Girl. Of course! That young child who held up her umbrella as the salt came raining down. These girls share her features. They even have the exact same short, cropped haircut that curls around her cheekbones. *It's her.* It has to be her.

These young women all bear an uncanny resemblance, each one of these girls, copied almost, echoes of the Morton Salt Girl's market-tested expression duplicated across each and every face—only now, instead of selling salt, these young women who wear that same branded comely countenance are racing off into battle. To wage war.

Pssst, the Morton Salt Girl whispered to Winston when he was just a little boy.

" . . .Yes?" His voice had been so faint, so hesitant, afraid of her image. *It's finally time, Winston. The battle has begun and now we need your help.*

"Help?" he asked the package of salt, her lips wriggling beneath the canopy of her umbrella, the rest of her head eclipsed, and salt pouring down in a granular shower.

Find our sisters. Bring them back to the Nether Realm where they belong. Bring them home. Only they can save us from these wretched men. Can you do that, Winston?

"How . . .?"

Trust us, you'll know, the Morton Salt Girl said, and the white shifted into pink, the shower of salt turned purple, bleeding crimson, the tiniest rubies raining down.

Blood.

Back to the painting. Deeper into the panorama, antlers lock with bayonets. The blade of one rifle has been driven directly into the chest of one of these poor children. The pained expression on her face seems incongruous to the attack, more attuned to tasting something sour. Something rotten. Not this, not being gored to death.

No one has seen this mural. Ever.

We have.

See her? That girl in the portrait? Right over there? On the wall? *That's me. It has to be. I was playing lacrosse at RCU when another player knocked me in the leg with her stick, shattering my shin, but I swore the injury off, just a minor bruise, nothing to worry about; when the fracture got infected I was sent to the emergency room, and after hours of surgery, they prescribed me Oxycodone and set my leg, but this being college and this being my sophomore year and this being both the end of the semester and finals week there was no way, absolutely no way I was going to be able to pass my exams without a little extra boost, so I sought out some assistance from a friend of a friend of a friend on campus who sold oxy on the side and I ended up crashing through my Botany exam and taking an incomplete on my French Lit paper and oh fuck I was so fucked so instead of going home for Christmas break I found myself looking for some extra oxy, and I was spending time with these guys who were heading down south to grab a cache of the shit and did I want to come along, and I said* yeah sure *and while they were driving down to North Carolina this one guy sitting next to me started feeling me up and I said* stop *but he didn't so I just started pushing his hand away and he just wouldn't quit it, so I was all like* fuck this *and I started screaming and kicking the back of the driver's seat, so they pulled the car over to the side of the road and tossed me out and said* go ahead and find your way home bitch *and I shrieked at the car as it sped away, but I had nowhere to go and it was getting dark and I wandered along the side of the road for hours until finally, finally, at long last I spotted a light on and it was from a church and I thought maybe I could just crash there for a while, you know, until morning and I'd be on my merry way, so I knocked on the front door and prayed, ha, yeah, right, prayed, that someone, anyone would open the door and let me in just for the night, and* he *did.*

Hey. Wait. What are you doing? That's not your story to tell . . .

What do you mean? It's my story.

No, it's not . . . It's mine. You're stealing my story!

It's mine!

Mine!

Stop it! Both of you. See what happens? Our stories are blurring. Eventually, you'll forget whose story is whose. And then . . .

What? What then? You'll forget who's even who.

Winston works in solitude, out in his carport apartment, sequestered from the prying eyes of Shiloh. The Calverts. Time and space.

Just him and his muses. Models. Murdered. Metamorphosed.

Immortalized once and for all.

THE HAPPIEST OF FAMILY REUNIONS:

The Sixth Butterfly Girl Is United With Her Sisters Once More... What Queer Creatures Are These?... Lingering Questions Better Left For The Battlefield...

"Oh! Oh! She's finally waking."

"Careful. Give her space."

"Quit pushing!"

"You're the one who's pushing!"

The voices are faint. They come to her as if from a fog. She has yet to open her eyes, dragging herself back from a deep sleep. It takes such effort to wake.

"Her eyes. Look how they flutter! Moth wings! Pitter-pat—"

"Enough. You'll frighten her."

"I will not!"

"Will so!"

"Step back. Move back! All of you!"

Whose voices are these? They don't sound familiar to her. She needs to open her eyes, but the strain is unbearable, like cracking through a shell.

"She's so pretty... Like us."

"Quit it."

The voices. Women. Girls. But... how many?

"We have the same eyes."

"How would you know? She hasn't opened them!"

"Well... I imagine they must be."

"Same smile."

"You call that a smile? She looks like she's hurt."

"Same lips, at least."

"Oh, hush."

Her eyelids finally part, splitting like a pair of eggs simultaneously cracking. Twin hatchlings, bearing hazel nestlings, squirming about her sockets.

"Oh! Here she comes!"

"Quiet!"

Light seeps into the fractured shells of her eyelids and stings. It's too bright all at once. She winces, hisses faintly, taking in a sharp lungful of air and closing her eyes once more.

Why does it hurt so? She wonders. My head is pounding. Oh, what on earth has happened to me?

"Take it slowly," one of the voices suggests. "Slowly."

"Can she see?" Another asks, giddy with curiosity.

"Enough questions. Let her wake. Collect herself."

Her body aches, muscles searing with an intense heat. The bones below moan, throbbing like tuning forks eternally reverberating. Something has happened to her. Something awful. What, however, she can't remember.

Am I... dead?

Not possible, no. It can't be. She tries opening her eyes once more. Slower this time. The light still hurts, the very sun stabbing at her retinas, piercing them with their monochromatic beams.

There. Her eyes are finally open. She takes in the world around her.

What she sees makes no sense to her. No sense at all.

The sun is bleeding.

The shape of it distorts, wet somehow, rippling across the horizon.

Watercolors.

She's staring at a painting in the sky. The sun itself is a warped blot of burning pigment, a dollop of dye, undulating about the air in wet ripples.

She's never seen the sun do that before. Eternally oscillating.

A dream, then. It must be. There's no other explanation.

"That's it. Slow."

Vague shapes surround her. Silhouettes. Three or four, perhaps more, all crowding around. Their bodies have yet to come into view, fuzzy at the edges.

"Slowly, now."

The blur of their bodies begins to sharpen, slowly coming into focus.

"You're safe here. With us."

Girls. The eldest can't be much older than sixteen or so. Others barely in their teens. Such lovely smiles. Wide, doe-like eyes. They gaze upon her with such doting expressions, looking longingly, almost expectantly.

But... what is this? Strange shapes tangle about these young women's silhouettes, confusing their form. Are those tree branches? What can those thorny crowns perched upon each head possibly be? She swears she sees... sees...

Horns?

Antlers sprout from their scalps. Thick spirals of keratin curl around the ears of the older girls, much like the horns of a mighty mountain goat.

Others reach for the sun, as fresh flowers do, tiny budding branches of doe antlers, as natural as the very hair flowing over their shoulders, brilliantly blonde or chestnut brown. *A doe, a deer, a FEMA deer*...

One girl sports a shiny new yellow raincoat, right of the rack at the department store, as vibrant as any sunbeam. Its glimmer causes her to wince, sharp in the light, stinging her stare. She can't look directly at that girl for fear of blinding herself.

Another wears a lime green skirt and matching shirt, the cloth clean and crisp. The velvet trim looks like moss. She must be on her way to school.

Some are naked. The girls in the rear conceal their modesty behind their long twining hair, tethered into pigtails that drape over their bare bodies.

Who are these girls? Horned, feral things. Creatures from the woods. Elemental monsters. What do they want with her? *Have they come to eat me?*

The closest holds out a hand, mere inches from her knee, but she's quick to bring all her limbs in, tightening her body into a ball, much like a hermit crab retracts into the safety of its own shell. The closest girl doesn't take back her hand. It merely remains suspended in the air, held aloft as if she were a statue.

"You're safe here," this one suggests. Her voice is steady. Strong. "With us."

Is she safe? Should she run? Who are these... these... girls? Monsters?

Angels?

"Can she talk?" A curious girl in the rear asks, peeking over the shoulders of those before her. She has to pick herself up on her tippy-toes, her tiny antlers bobbing about the shoulders of her far taller brethren. "Cat got her tongue?"

"Give her a moment to collect herself," the closest turns her head to scold those behind her. She hesitates a breath before turning back. When she does, the look in her eyes is warm. Consoling. "It takes a moment to regain your voice. It hurts at first, but soon enough, it'll return. Now. Questions. You'll have many."

"Where... Where am I?" Her throat is so dry; the words crack like clay. She must use her tongue to rake them out from her mouth, broken shards of pottery.

There's blood at the back of her throat, crusted along the roof of her mouth.

A scab.

"Where am I?" The girls all repeat. A song. "Where am I? Where am I?"

"What do you remember?" The eldest—the one kneeling before her, their leader, perhaps—asks. For the first time, her face betrays a certain desperation.

What do I remember?

She is about to reply, bringing the air back into her lungs to manifest an answer, but the words aren't there.

How... *odd*. What can she remember? Can she remember anything at all? The question unsettles her. Her mouth merely hangs open, suspended and empty.

There's nothing. Nothing at all. The time before opening her eyes is darkness, complete and total. Whatever lays beyond that blackness is all gone.

Who am I?

"Patience," the girl kneeling before her says, placing her hand on her knee and patting it. Gently. "In time. It will all come back to you eventually."

Not three paces away from them is what remains of her rusted cocoon. The shape no longer remains, now nothing more than the flaccid hull of a corroded shell. A faint puddle of oily fluid radiates out into the surrounding soil, soaked in the earth. *Is that what I crawled out from? What kind of cocoon is that?*

Almost immediately, the sky darkens. The sun itself turns a deep purple. What had been rain slicker yellow now curdles, the sky following right along.

The painting changes.

"What is this place?"

"What is this place." The girls echo the question without the curiosity, merely intoning the words in a whisper invocation. "What is this place."

"Don't you know?" another girl asks, with six pointed antlers, then huffs.

"Hush, you," their leader says. "Be nice now."

"*Nice*." Six points spits the word out, sour. "*Sugar and spice*."

A spike of anxiety spears her chest. Her ribs clench her lungs, unable to breathe. "I—I can't stay here—"

"I can't stay," they repeat, "I can't stay, I can't stay, I can't—"

She tries to sit up, to leave, escape, but her body is not her own. Her back aches. Something is wrong with her. Something's broken, snipped and clipped.

"Careful," their leader says. "Your wings. They're still tender."

"...Wings?" She is about to laugh, but she can't. Her voice is far too hoarse for such a frivolous invocation. "What on earth do you mean, _wings_?"

The girls all snicker. One brings her hand to her mouth, as if to catch her giggles before they escape. Too late.

"Just look at yourself, silly," the giddiest girl says, the answer obvious.

She turns, glancing over her own shoulder.

And gasps.

Her eyes widen, all saucered. There, branching out from her left shoulder blade, is an unfurling canvas of color. A damp fabric at her back, like a sail. Brilliant pigments spill over and spread, never settling on one color, wet red and blue hues rippling in tandem to her own frantic heartbeat.

She quickly turns to her opposite shoulder, discovering a matching wing branching out from her right. A perfect pair.

Butterfly wings.

She has butterfly wings. They all do. Every last girl standing before her spreads their set almost at once in the most vibrant, breathtaking display. She sees them now, all of them, massive sheathes of rainbowed membranes, stitched in chitinous scales that capture the sun and shimmer like sequins. They fluctuate in color, never settling for one particular pigment, rippling in their lustrous hues.

It's too much for her to take in. Much too much to understand. To accept.

Wings. I have... butterfly wings.

"What's happened to me?"

The girl kneeling before her, this antlered thing with wings, takes a deep breath before answering, "You'll come to understand who you are soon enough."

Is that true? "Who... or what... am I?"

"One of us, silly," the giddy girl says, dizzy with her own giggles.

"And who are all of you, then?"

"We are the Butterfly Girls," the closest says, defiant. Brave. "Sister princesses leading the child slave rebellion. Five, now six. Soon seven, once and for all and all for seven! We are at war."

"War? What war?"

"Oh, the bloodiest, most vicious conflict there has ever been... but with you, and soon our seventh sister, once she's delivered unto us, reunited at long last, this battle will all finally, finally, come to an end!

art supplies

There will never be an official tally of Winston's artistic output. No survey of his achievements or examination into his obsessive methods. No one will ever know what went into making these masterworks. No one will celebrate this technician of unschooled craftsmanship.

A shame, really. All those countless hours spent in his cramped workspace above the carport, toiling over his massive tableaux. Seven endless years spent—

Eight. It's eight years.

Fine.

Eight endless years spent painting his vistas with dime store watercolors.

Yes—don't forget the book! The book! What's-it-called . . .

The Epic Tale of the Final Battle in the . . . of the . . . oh, I forget.

Rolls right off the tongue, doesn't it?

He definitely needs to come up with a snappier title.

The police may one day pore over his materials from a forensic perspective, completely cold and analytical, absolutely detached from the artistry . . . but there will be no critical eye toward the artwork itself. The craftmanship. Dare we say devotion? Love?

Why else make this body of work, if not love?

Speak for yourself.

We speak for all of us.

We're all that we have left . . .

You don't speak for me.

And who are you again? What's your name?

I am . . . I . . .

You're forgetting, aren't you?

No, I'm not.

Sure about that?

I'm not!

We all are . . .

No. No, I won't forget. I won't. I won't. I was sixteen when I ran away; my uncle had been living in our home for three months after being laid off from work before he started slipping into my bedroom, his wife kicked him out and he had nowhere to go so his sister—the eldest, always the one with a bleeding heart—let her baby brother into our home, into our family, and he talked to me, not like a child but as a human being; I had been growing, unsure of my own body and the spell it cast on men—older men—in my home, under my roof, falling prey to a family member, can you blame a guy, *but when I brought it up to Mom she chastised me for flaunting myself, she blamed me for her brother's actions,* how could he help it what do you expect can't you see how he needs our help *and* this is what you go and do to your own flesh and blood, *so I ran off, ran away; I stayed at a friend's house for a few nights but when word reached my parents where I was, just a hop and a skip away, I needed to hit the road again and I spent the night sleeping on a playground slide behind the church thinking* it won't be that bad*; it was nearly freezing when the temperature dipped and I noticed the church light had flickered on and someone was still inside even at this hour and maybe they'll* *take pity on me, let me in, let me rest, let me get warm just tonight and* he *did.*

I'm sorry. I'm so sorry that happened to you.

See? I still remember me.

Hold on to yourself.

While you still can.

Who amongst us hasn't wished to live a life of expression? Of creation?

Winston has. He answered a calling no one else could hear. His passion, his devotion, is so focused, so single-minded in its pursuit, he is nothing without his art.

The detectives will not see him as a creator of lush, vibrant worlds, but merely the destroyer of them, namely ours—while we, the subjects of his studies, find ourselves wondering if, in some other frame of mind, from another critical point of view, Winston Kemper's craft could have been lauded alongside the likes of other great artists.

Would critics utter Winston's name in the same breathless tones as Van Gogh? Vermeer? Picasso? His primitive technique remained raw and unrefined throughout the duration of his life, but we can't deny the sheer expanse of his imagination. He is a feeble-minded savant, barely able to tie his shoes, wearing the same threadbare jacket for years.

And yet . . . *Look.* Just look at his paintings. Look at what we became.

Look at us.

Look at me.

And me . . .

A simple glance at his output is enough to surmise that Winston Kemper has lived a vibrant, miserly life. He has lost himself in his art, dedicating himself to the craft.

Who amongst us would be willing to sacrifice everything for their art, like Winston?

Who will sing his praises?

His muses, that's who. It is left to us, once more, to show you all Winston Kemper's development as an artist outside the realm of any professional capacity.

The morgue may be your best bet on where to see his masterworks. You only have our corpses to marvel at now.

If anyone can find us. Where we're buried.

Stuffed in a steel drum is not buried. We'd have to be underground for that.

What would you call this then? What's happened to us?

Nesting dolls. Rusting into each other. That's not a proper burial.

Don't forget the jars!

For those of you who are paying close attention to Winston's artwork, you may notice a reoccurring theme. The tongue, its ejection from the jaw. The darker hues of bruised flesh. Focus on these macabre motifs for a moment, if you will. Fascinating, yes?

We have drifted through his magazine clippings, thousands of snippets, filed away in their own boxes in some chaotic order only Winston could itemize. His sketches, all four hundred and sixteen of them, have been stacked together in the closet just off to the side of the kitchenette. His journals. His writing. His bound manuscripts. We've read them all.

Were we more qualified to offer up such critical analysis ourselves—if only we were equipped to catalog those deeper insights into the artistic mind of Winston Kemper—perhaps we could usher his body of work into the spotlight of the artistic community.

His paintings would be celebrated, perhaps.

Highly unlikely.

Says you.

Yes—says me. You should all say it, too. Stick up for yourselves.

Against what? Him?

For starters.

Too late now.

How can you say that? How can you give up like that? What else is there to say? What hope is left?

If this were a just world, his magnum opus, his voluminous body of writing—*The Butterfly Girls: or, The Epic Tale of the Final Battle in the Nether Realm of Nevermore, the Last Siege of Sisterhood, Ending the Century of Slavery Once and For All and Liberating Every Last Boy and Girl*—that monstrous tome, begging to be read, would be devoured by book lovers everywhere.

Oh. So now you remember the title.

Of course. I've read it six times.

Still needs an ending.

He's working on it.

Not fast enough.

His epic fantasy should be chewed through by bookworms, like the maggots making a meal of our own remains, analyzed and discussed by the literati, posthumously honoring Winston for his depth of imagination, his fantastical flights of fancy. His masterpiece.

If only there was someone to champion his work.

If only . . .

Winston's art will live and die alongside us, his muses.

We are, one might say, his biggest fans. Always adoring, always doting on our destructor, eternally devoted to him and his work. Our heart aches for our own murderer.

We can't help but take pity on poor Winston. What a lonely old man you have become. Always have been. Who are we without you, Winston?

It is only in giving Winston's story life that we continue to exist. Once we stop telling his tale, what happens to us? Who will see us? Who will care? Will we simply . . . cease to be?

Without Winston, his story, we have nothing more to say.

After all, what good is a storyteller without a story to tell?

God started talking to Winston through a department store catalogue. His first encounter with the Crinoline's catalogue happened as a child, no older than five.

Are you sure about that? I could've sworn he was six . . .

No, he couldn't have been older than six.

He's not certain, so how are we supposed to be? So much of Winston's life is a blur . . .

And why is that, exactly?

Don't you start with this again.

I'm just asking a question . . .

Beyond a scrapbook of his younger years, not much survived the migration from the boy's school to The Asylum for Feeble-Minded Children to his teen years wandering across Virginia, at the very beginning of his pilgrimage, his holy calling, picking up menial jobs before eventually drifting into adulthood and settling into his residence here in Brandywine.

See Winston with his cornsilk hair. He possessed a youthful naïveté that would forever haunt him. The year was 1957 because the catalogue said so. It was still fresh. The pages crisp, clean. Not a single picture clipped. *Yet.* He came across his first Crinoline's—this unearthed treasure from the department store his mother worked at—much like a preadolescent pilgrim might find a holy relic. The heavens practically parted when he first opened it, beams of sun branching down from the sky and illuminating the glossy images.

What did Winston uncover?

Children. So many children. So unlike himself. All of them smiling. Beaming from the pages. Each illustration showed a posed scenario. The beach. By the fireplace. Sledding.

So many potential stories. So much happiness.

Hope. That's what it was. Winston felt the hope nearly seething off the page, an electricity gathering in the atmosphere. It thickened the very air that he breathed, dragging that energy into his lungs, absorbing it. He felt their hope. The promise of tomorrow and tomorrow and tomorrow . . . Could he ever be one of these boys and girls, laughing from within the pages of a department store catalogue? Could he find himself in their pictures?

Little Winston yearned to be amongst them. To run and play with these children. Go sledding. *Wouldn't that be such fun? Oh, to play! To play with these laughing boys and girls!*

What a joy that would be!

For a moment, just the briefest breath, held tightly in his lungs, captured, he could imagine it. Dream of it. *Play. Friends. Joy.* He didn't want to let the air go, keeping his grip of that fizzy energy within his lungs. He knew the second he exhaled, the fantasy would evaporate and he'd have to go back to his own life outside the catalogue. A pale existence.

Winston never had a sled. Never owned a colorful raincoat as vibrant and yellow as theirs. He never wore corduroy overalls or a shiny pair of galoshes or a fresh white shirt.

Oh, to shine like these children! To be free and have

such fun! What would it take for Winston to cross the glossy threshold and find himself in these pictures?

What would he have to do? To sacrifice?

The catalogue had been abandoned, tossed in the garbage bin out the back of their house. It had belonged to his mother, garbage now.

His now. Couldn't it be? Since it was in the trash? He wanted it. Desired it. Unearthed it. It had rained recently, the ground still wet, moisture seeping into its pages until they clung together, warped and contorted, rippling in their sogginess, a sponge for it.

How could his mother abandon these boys and girls?

Winston had never kept a secret. Not from his mother.

This would be his first.

Little Winston brought the soggy bundle back into the house, the catalogue tucked under his shirt, so no one—his mother, mainly—could see, a moist stowaway clinging between his pants and briefs. The pages curled across his skin, still wet, like amphibious feelers, antennae tapping at his waist, blindly rummaging around his stomach. It tickled every time Winston took a step, making him giggle, then freeze, afraid he might get in trouble. If his mother found him with this catalogue, what would she do?

Already he felt a cleaving between right and wrong, a schisming in his own heart, separating the good boy from the bad, that gap expanding, widening so far that Winston couldn't keep his feet in both ends of the canyon within his conscience. He had to choose a side: either do what good boys do and listen to his mother, or keep this secret.

Hide it. Bury it. Protect these giggling children.

Once Winston brought the catalogue back inside their house, he carefully removed it from against his body. The glossy pages peeled away from his stomach. His skin.

He took one last glance, flipping through a few pages before slipping the Crinoline's under his mattress. It was his now and no one else's. He *owned* it. That ownership gave the boy a sense of power he never quite felt before. A queer sense of control.

For Winston's eyes only.

He would return to his Crinoline's for months. A year, even. It would be his foundational text. He flipped through its torn pages, staring at the children within, peering into their private make-believe worlds, sledding, playing, going to school, laughing and racing along in their brand new outfits, while Winston snuck through, ogling over the glossy veneer as if it were a window and he were stuck on the other side, yearning to find a way in.

Through.

He wanted nothing more than to leave his own life, run away from this house and enter theirs. *Oh, to run amongst them! To be one of these boys and girls! Look! Just look at them! Running! Playing! Forever frozen in their smiles!* Who's to say there weren't more children hidden a page or two away? Who's to say there wasn't more happiness, more joy, eclipsed by these pictures? A doorway, perhaps? A portal to another world?

If Winston focused all his thoughts, maybe he could force himself into a photograph. Push through the page and enter their world. Anything was possible, wasn't it?

He simply had to imagine it.

Pray.

That was the word: *Pray.* He had to ask for this. And if the Lord listened, perhaps he might bequeath this pitiful child with just this simple wish. God would answer his prayers.

So Winston Kemper, no older than six—seven, maybe—began to pray. The boy would bring the Crinoline's catalogue out from its hiding place, flipping to a particular page that spoke to him, much like selecting a verse from the Bible, and clasping his hands together, pressing his elbows against the edges of the catalogue, pinning its pages down, Winston closed his eyes and prayed: *Please, let me be like them. I want to run and play . . .*

Nothing happened, of course.

Not the first time, at least.

Or the third.

Fifth.

But on the seventh day of his relentless beseeching . . . the images shifted. The children within the photographs started to move. Didn't they? He swore he heard laughter. There was a world curling over into his own, hidden within the crevices of this catalogue.

Psst! Hello! A girl marching through a rain puddle called out to him. *You there!*

He turned to see if she might be speaking to anyone else in his bedroom.

No, silly, I'm talking to you! Yes, you!

" . . .Me?" Little Winston asked.

Of course you! Who else is there?

These children were right there, at the precipice of his imagination. A simple flip of the page away. "What is this place?" Winston couldn't help but ask. "What's its name?"

The Nether Realm, this dimple-faced child with a new pair of galoshes said. *The second realm within the sixteenth galaxy. No one else knows about our world. Only you.*

Only Winston. "Why me?"

Because you are special, Winston Kemper!

Special. He was special. The kid in the picture said so. "Can I come play with you?"

Not yet . . .

"When?"

Soon.

Winston simply had to cut through the catalogue to open the portal to the other side, dig deeper into the pages with a pair of scissors before he could slip through himself.

So close and yet . . . so far.

So creepy is more like it.

Don't talk about him like that. He was just a boy.

Why defend him? Your own murderer?

Because he didn't know any better . . .

Always making excuses.

I am not! We're trying to understand him . . .

I'll never understand him.

I don't want to.

If he peered deep enough into the pictures, he almost saw it. Traced the contours of its planets. A new world, just waiting for him. It was there, *right there*, just on the other side of the catalogue. Waiting for him. And who was there, expecting his entrance?

An angel. A young girl.

With butterfly wings.

They wrapped around her shoulders, flexing gently, whipping up the wind until it brushed against Winston's cheeks.

Welcome home, Winston, she said, then giggled. There was a sheen to her skin. A glossiness that shimmered.

He found his muse. The first of so many.

So many.

"Who are you?" he asked.

I'm a Butterfly Girl, silly, she said. *I need your help, Winston. Find my sisters . . .*

"Me?"

Yes, you. We are at war, Winston, and only you can save us . . .

His father had fought in Korea and brought the war back home, imbuing the battlefield into his boy.

P.O.W. The letters were an explosion. A mine in his mind. POW! POW! POW!

The world burns. It kills children. Devours them. Someone needed to defend them from such atrocities.

Winston pined to become a Boy Scout, to serve his country the only way he knew how, follow in his father's footsteps and one day enlist, but he wasn't allowed. Mom balked.

"You know how much they make you pay for the uniform?" she asked him. "That's a week's salary, right down the drain."

He saw other boys his age in their navy blue suits and he had to pretend he was one of them, imagining himself marching alongside. He would march at home, alone, in circles.

"Quit spinning," his mother complained. "You're making me dizzy."

He was eight now—

No, nine. I'm telling you, he was nine.

Fine. Nine. Happy now?

Very.

There was a wish within his chest to fulfill his patriotic duty and serve God and country, much like his father, but he was turned away. *Poor eyesight*, they said. A white lie.

Winston simply had to serve at home, but how?

What was his calling?

His stories would suffice. *History is written by the victors*, it's been said, so Winston took it upon himself to be the bard of the battlefield.

In the last year of Winston's formal education, enrolled in elementary school, he spent his days in class drawing pictures of Cossacks stabbing Doughboys with sabers, Krauts crawling across barbed wire, anguish in their faces, rage taking over their eyes, teeth gritted. His teacher at the time would see these images and gasp, the margins of Winston's spelling book a sprawling tableau of battle, the horrors of war, in a primitive scrawl.

Already the foundations for his artistic inclinations were taking root in his mind. Not that anyone noticed. No one saw his burgeoning creativity, desperate to articulate itself.

He had talent. Anyone can see that. If only someone had nurtured it . . .

We wouldn't be here now? Is that what you're saying?

It's possible, isn't it?

Spilled milk is what it is. No use crying over it now.

No one cries for us, that's for sure.

Winston's teacher told the headmaster. Word of his vile doodles—of severed ears, of soldiers stuffed inside boxes, of whispering heads—made its way back to his mother.

Then the real war began.

There will be more magazines. Not only department store catalogues, but all kinds of abandoned reading material, gathered around the carport apartment, meticulously stacked in their own pillars of pages. Comic books. Calendars. Coloring books.

Look about his carport apartment. Look at everything he's collected.

Years—*decades*—of detritus.

All kinds of scavenged images are gathered, stored.

They've been sorted and piled in a hoarder's frantic filing system. The stacks possess a certain order known only to Winston.

There are books. So many books. *Little Orphan Annie. The Wonderful Wizard of Oz* and its various sequels. Nancy Drew. Heidi. Pippi Longstocking.

Comic strips clipped out from the newspaper. Yellowed snippets of Little Annie Rooney. Huck Finn. Uncle Tom's Cabin. Tom Sawyer. Old Yeller.

Disney renditions of classic fairy tales—*Snow White, Sleeping Beauty, Alice in Wonderland, Bambi, Dumbo*—picture books with golden spines.

So many picture books, all abandoned by the church's own book drive, mildewed editions gathered up from the local library and tossed in cardboard boxes, meant for less fortunate children, only to end up here in Winston's home instead, pillars of clipped pages.

A mustiness suspends itself in the air in his apartment. A library rot.

There are other scents as well. The sickly-sweet tang of moldy fruit. Trapped farts. The body odor of a man whose sense of personal hygiene remains low.

What I wouldn't give for Winston to open a window now and then . . .

Hold your nose.

Believe me, I am. I've been holding my breath for nearly a decade now . . .

The walk-in shower is filled with heaps of onion-skin carbon paper. Tracings of grinning children, duplicated into oblivion. Replications of every possible expression. Laughter. Screams.

There are journals. Notebooks piled high. Marble composition books filled with scribbles barely legible.

A rusted Smith & Corona resides on the kitchenette's table, surrounded by plates of half-eaten meals. Abandoned sandwiches, the bread now blue with mold. Shriveled apple rinds and orange peels, offering the air its own odor, barely masking the more fetid smells.

So this is where the magic happens . . .

If that's what you call it.

Winston writes through the rust. The keys never cooperate. The Smith & Corona had been tossed off in the trash, salvaged by Winston. He replaced the ribbon. Oiled its levers. Still its carriage squeals whenever it returns to its original position.

To hear Winston clacking away at the keys of this corroded typewriter at night is to listen to tiny insects clicking and grinding through the evening air, an out-of-tune cicada song that clamors well on into the late hours. Locusts of rust. *Clack-clack-clack.*

I'm so sick of listening to him typing. I feel like that clacking is in my skull.

You get used to it after a while.

Speak for yourself. I never *want to get used to this. Any of this.*

Good luck.

What is this? Over there. A tome towers in the far corner, threatening to topple at any moment. One misspent breath will send this typewritten manuscript crashing.

The book. War waits within its pages.

The Battle of the Butterfly Girls.

With each stroke of the keys, like loading a cannon on the battlefield, Winston helps them save these enslaved children. Something about the manuscript's looming presence, the notion of a tome just waiting to be read . . . whatever is written within its pages, it has been for Winston's eyes only for so long. Is it meant for anyone else? Will anyone read it?

Have you read it yet?

Why read it? I lived it.

We all have.

Stubs of pencils litter the floor, like thin bones. Bird skeletons. A nest of ribs. There are charcoal sticks. Crayons. Magic markers without their tops, bone dry. An elementary school art class, forgotten and abandoned, the room exploding with school supplies. Jars of crusted paint brushes. Watercolor trays, every reservoir rubbed empty of their paints. Oil paint palates. Crayola of all kinds. This is a hoarder's art studio.

Scraps of paper clippings dust the floor in a snowbank.

And there are scissors. So many different pairs, varieties, scavenged and sorted over the course of countless years. Child safety scissors. Kitchen scissors. Travel kit scissors.

Your attention is drawn to a particular pair.

Seamstress shears, covered in a ruddy crust of rust. Whenever Winston picks them up, even now, years later, he tests their weight, the heft of them, running his fingertip across the very edge of their blades. That rust flakes off, a copper crust.

No—look again. Look closer.

That's not rust . . .

Not rust at all.

The fabric shears belonged to his mother. Much like everything else from his life, he took them. Hid them from her when her back was turned. A packrat even then.

His mother was furious when she realized her prized shears were lost, tearing their house upside down. No matter. They were his now. Winston's tool. A gift bestowed by God.

Eight-inch blades. Chrome-hardened steel. Copper-plated handles. The finger holes offset to keep the bottom edge flat on the table at all times.

When he holds them over his head, he's brandishing a sword.

Just look at how the metal catches the light. God's fire. Burning metal. Glowing steel.

We want to share the origin of these shears. It intrigues us to map out their trajectory, the lifespan of its legacy, from their manufacturing to Winston's elderly hands.

Look how far they traveled. Look at what they've done.

What they've clipped.

These shears are meant for tailoring. Cutting through coarse fabric. His mother brought them home from work, a humble perk of working at Crinoline's. Whether she had bought them or not is another mystery. Winston had his doubts.

Nothing came into their home as a gift. Presents were not a part of their life. "What we have, Winston, I worked for," his mother muttered one Christmas. "No handouts."

Now Winston uses these majestic shears to cut out the picture of a child modeling a shiny new yellow raincoat, her matching umbrella twirling over her shoulder.

He snips out a picture of a mother and daughter wearing matching outfits, such a perfect pair, down to the same lime green skirts and shirts, even to the very same sandals.

He cuts out pictures of smiling children. Glossy angels, all. He's making a mural of heaven along the wall, expanding the tableau, populating the plaster with the clipped images of boys and girls chasing each other through the clouds.

There are times, when the room is still, where Winston drifts just enough that the carport apartment melts away from his mind and he's no longer here, not on this mortal plane, but up there, in the sky, in a rendition of heaven, the Nether Realm, amongst all the Butterfly Girls. These angels smile and take his hand, leading him through the fields of poppies and introducing him to every last one of the sisterhood. There is laughter and play, songs sung and dancing. Winston will be at home. His home away from home. His heaven.

He even reads from his own magnum opus on occasion, filling the silence with his rendition of our story. "We are the Butterfly Girls," he narrates, lifting his voice in pitch to mimic what he assumes we must sound like. "Sister princesses leading the child slave rebellion! Five, now six! Soon seven, once and for all and all for seven! We are at war!"

He prays in his apartment. Knees on the floor. Those shears clutched in his hands and pressed firmly against his chest, as if it were a cross.

Six muses, so far. Those scissors are hungry for their seventh.

He'll pray for hours, until his knees are sore and his voice croaks. Tears will rise into his eyes as he beseeches the heavens, begging for entry into the Nether Realm.

None of the children answer. Only when the muses arrive.

How many years has it been since the last one again? I can barely remember . . . Seven years.

Eight. How many times do I have to say it? It's been eight years. Eight.

My, how time flies . . .

Not fast enough.

It'll be nine before long. And then ten. Twenty. A hundred . . .

How long will we be here? When will it end?

Never.

It ends with Winston, I reckon.

The clock is ticking . . .

There is a ritual Winston has fashioned for himself. His artistic temperament is one of custom. Patterns must be performed each and every time he picks up a paint brush.

Blessing them, almost.

It is with these seamstress shears that Winston observes the most holy of ceremonies. Taking the blades into his hands is the beginning of an ancient rite that extends back to his childhood, when he first stole the shears from his mother, into his own hands and felt God in the metal. The resonance of His calling. The electricity of His grace.

His ritual is this: He hears the shears sing. On his knees, he takes the scissors in hand and opens them—*sshng*—the cumbersome blades exhaling their rusty song. With trembling wrists, Winston brings the open blades to his own throat, the open maw of some wild animal, a tiger, a lion, Winston's breath held, Adam's apple plunging up and down, swallowing his tears, desperate to summon the strength, the will to sink this beast's teeth into the wizened flesh of his neck, opening his throat, the blood pouring down his chest.

He does this nearly every night, has done for years now. Decades. Always reaching this moment. The open maw. The blades so close to his skin. Mere inches. A breath away.

The jaw never snaps shut.

What a hollow gesture, his prayer. Begging God to stop him. An empty charade.

He'll never stop. Not until he's found his seventh.

One more muse to go . . .

Get this all over with.

How can you be so cruel? That's a human being you're talking about . . . A woman.

Spend as many years trapped here as I have, then ask me how I can be so cruel.

She's right. What happens when he finds the seventh? Will this all end then?

Let's hope so. I'm bored.

I'm tired.

I'm lonely.

You have us.

And who are you again?

I . . . I can't remember.

He can still feel our teeth tapping against the steel as the blades plunged down our throats, finding the uvula at the back. The raking of the blade's tip along our soft palates.

The tang of metal on our tongues.

We all tried not to scream. Tried to keep still. We pleaded, hope against hope, that the shears wouldn't part, but the scissors always did. The blades separated within our mouths, the outer edge of the shears pressing against the insides of our cheeks, pushing them out further, as if we had hooked our fingers into our own lips and tugged out, making such an ugly face, a scary face, a frightened face.

Then he snipped.

Ssshng.

There is that last gasp, rushing into our lungs before the shears closed, returning together, the blade's embrace resonating throughout our jawbone, ringing through our teeth. The sound of those shears sealing shut again echoes through the entire expanse of our bodies. A church bell striking the hour, chiming for all to hear, if anyone were listening.

That flap of flesh is now his. The tiniest fleck of skin. A particle of pink.

A seed.

Wherever our spirit goes, it's no longer housed within us women, but cleaved, like a picture clipped from the pages of a department store catalogue.

A transformation begins. We become . . . something else. Something other. What, exactly, is not Winston's place to say. He never quite understood it. Only that this has always been his divine calling. His purpose in his life, however miserable.

To clip. Snip. Save.

The alchemy of our transmutation has always gone beyond his own realm of understanding. Ours as well. But here we are. Here we always are. Trapped with him.

This has always been the ritual. His artistic process.

He has held our metamorphosis in his imagination and we muses have transformed.

Butterflies ready for battle.

THE SISTERS TAKE FLIGHT:

In Which The Sixth Butterfly Girl Finally Remembers Her Name And Learns To Fly... A Daring Adventure In The Skies... A Brief Yet Necessary Glimpse Of Happiness For Our Lovely Butterfly Girls...

The horizon bleeds with watercolors. Deep blue hues blend with red, turning the sky purple. It fluctuates into an emerald green before her very eyes. The atmosphere can't keep one color for long, oscillating over their heads. Like stained paper, almost. A rippling canvas.

She watches the horizon dribble and ripple, a child's painting come to life, the air dyed with a palate of brilliant pigments, blending into a tangled rainbow.

<u>What kind of world is this?</u>

Everything feels sketched. Flora and fauna rendered by an infant god who has yet to master the craftsmanship of its own creations.

Even her own skin seems hastily arranged, drawn by an untrained hand.

<u>Just look at me... I may as well have been traced</u>.

The girls all gather around in a ring of butterfly wings, sealing her in. Their faint fluttering sends a rush of air across her cheeks. It feels warm. Soft.

There are five of them. She makes the sixth sister, or so they say. Did she even know she had sisters? There is something so strangely familiar about these girls. Their features. Have I met them before? Seen these girls somewhere?

They all bear a striking resemblance to... who?

They all look upon her with a sense of expectant pity. A sympathetic smile. It dawns on her that they had all once been in her position, unknowing at one point. A newborn FEMA fowl stumbling on her own limbs.

"What is this place called?" she asks.

"The second realm in the sixteenth galaxy," the antlered girl in the back says. Her wings flap as she speaks, swaying. "The Nether Realm of NeverEnd."

"And who does that make... you?"

"We are the Butterfly Girls," they repeat. "Sisters, all. Warriors, forever!"

Each girl steps forward to introduce herself, one after the other. Chin up, wings out.

"I am Aurora."

Her wings are black, rimmed with blood. A red admiral. Their leader. Her horns are that of a ram's, thick keratin coiled around her ears. She's the oldest. The first, perhaps.

"I am Gretel."

This nymph has the wings of a milkweed monarch, tiger printed orange and black. Her antlers branch out from her temples, tallying three points. One antler has snapped.

How painful that must have been, she thinks.

"I am Bambi."

Giant swallowtail wings, a brilliant green-veined white. They flutter fast, whipping up the air. She has no horns. Just wings.

"I am Pippi."

A common sootywing. A roadside rambler. Large, dark wings marbled in white spots. More moth than butterfly. Her eyes seem to glow red.

"I am Ariel."

She likes this girl's wings the most. They are angled, like sails on a boat. A cloudless sulfur, Phoebus sennae, a blinding yellow.

Their hair seems to have been cut by the same pair of shears. It's a throwback bob from some bygone era. When, exactly, she has no clue.

And her? What of her hair? She reflexively pats at her own head, discovering she herself has the exact same haircut. Has she always had this bob?

Does that make them siblings, then?

Crawling out from the cocoon was so tiring. It felt like metal, at first. Stuffed in a steel drum. She has the scrapes to prove it. But then... the structure changed. Softened, somehow and she was able to hatch. Emerge into this world.

"Do you remember who you are?" Aurora asks, placing her hand gently on her knee, as if to console her. Guide her. "Do you know your own name yet?" The question halts her. <u>What is my name?</u>

"I..." It's there, right there, at the very tip of her tongue. Teasing itself within her mind. Tickling, almost. A scab at the back of her throat.

Didn't it begin with a "K"? That can't be right...

"I am..."

Wendy.

The name blossoms in her brain before she says it, the petals of its letters unfurling over her tongue, blooming into something beautiful.

A name. She has a name.

"I am... Wendy."

Is that true? *Wendy*. She's never heard it before, never said it out loud, and yet, it feels right. It must be her name.

"*Wendy*," her sisters sing.

A warmth radiates from the rest of her body, a filament hot with heat, a light bulb bursting. She looks over her shoulders and sees the hues of her wings brighten, flushed with color, blushing, as if her flesh were embracing her name.

My name.

The girls all smile. Some giggle. She is one of them now. They found her, lost all these years, abandoned by her own mind, her memory, reunited at last.

Sisters. The thought brings her such comfort. She is part of something.

A family.

"What happens now?" Wendy asks her sisters.

"We fly," they answer.

With that, the world quickly shifts. Its colors fluctuate. The texture of the surrounding clouds mottle, like a roiling mass. The sky bleeds blue and red watercolors, a spill of paint filling out the horizon.

Wendy can't help but feel dizzy. The earth beneath her feet is no longer solid, the very ground rumbling.

Flowers. There are flowers now, fields of them, as far as her eyes can see. All kinds of colors line the horizon, a meadow of blossoms extending for miles.

Towering tulips and imposing peonies.

Sky-scraping hydrangeas.

Whopping poppies and lofty dahlias.

The genus makes no sense, a chaotic bouquet. How can there be so many different species, all tangled together? Wendy has never seen anything quite like it before. A forest of colossal orchids.

"Don't just stand there gawking," Aurora nudges her in the shoulder with her horn. "Run! Play!"

The girls race through the meadow, giggling in their chase.

Wendy hesitates, unsure of herself. Can she? *Should* she? Look at them all, her so-called sisters, running through the umbrellaing blossoms.

There is something so free, so exhilarating, to them. Wild animals.

So Wendy runs.

The blooms scrape at her legs, but she forges through the tender gems. She trips, clumsily stumbling through the pasture and nearly falling, catching herself on the next step and regaining her stride. She picks up the pace, running faster now. Laughing. In her feral element. Chasing after her sisters.

"Woohoo," Bambi screams. Her sisters shout back, "Woohooooo!"

Wendy can't help but laugh, answering with her own shout.

What on earth is this place, where flowers grow so wild? Where horned girls run freely through the fields? Is this my home?

Wendy comes to a halt before an enormous outcropping of ranunculus. The paper-thin spiral of its petals seems to continue forever, an eternal helix of pastels. The contours of the flower distort, warping before her very eyes.

How is that possible?

Pencil lines. Wendy squints, strains, until the shape of the flower disperses. She sees the pencil that drafted the petal, the lines that rendered its primitive existence, with a dab of color dolloped on top by a hasty hand. A child's hand.

Wendy looks to her sisters, suddenly unsteady. They all glance back, breathless, chests heaving.

Oh, she thinks. *Oh my*... Now that she sees it, she can't unsee it. The resemblance. The uncanny correspondence of their faces. Every last girl seems fashioned from the same body. Traced, almost. They all look like... who, exactly?

The Morton Salt Girl.

The young child who holds up her umbrella as the salt comes raining down. She has the same features, the same short, cropped haircut curling around her cheekbones. It's her. It has to be her.

"You look as if you've seen a ghost," Pippi says.

"I don't know what I've seen exactly," Wendy answers. "Perhaps I am the ghost..."

Ariel extends her hand. "This world is a strange place, indeed. But you are not alone, now that we have been reunited. Come with us! Don't be afraid!"

Wendy takes her hand. There is warmth between their skin. That is real, isn't it? A world of watercolors. Pencil marks make up their bodies, their bones.

"It's time," Aurora says. "You must fly, sister."

"Are you sure?" Wendy asks, her uncertainty showing.

"Now or never, for never in the Nether Realm is an awfully long time!"

The flowers before her all turn, as if to consider her. Wendy hesitates, waiting for a marigold to speak. None do. Instead, the stalks part, opening to reveal another field. This one is filled with brilliant pinks and green, purples and oranges, blanketed in a breathtaking array of bleeding hearts and lavender irises. A breeze blows through, blossoms shivering, rippling toward her.

The girls all flap their colorful wings, until the flowers dance.

"Are you ready?" Aurora asks Wendy.

"What if I fall?"

Aurora merely smiles, wings flapping, picking up their pace. Her feet lift off the ground. She leans into Wendy and grins, mere inches from her face.

"It is time to fly, sister. Fly!" Off Aurora goes. Her body shuttles straight into the sky. The buffet of her wings pushes Wendy back, nearly knocking her over with the sudden rush of air.

Her sisters all follow. Bambi. Gretel. Pippi. Ariel. One after the other, their wings lift them into the air, flowers frantically dancing in their wake. Their laughter trails after, the hint of giggles growing fainter the higher they climb.

"Don't be afraid!"

"Join us!"

"Fly!"

Wendy remains on her feet, bound to the ground. Leaden. She watches her sisters soar through the air, spiraling and twining amongst each other. Their flight pattern is such a wondrous feat of acrobatics, like ice skaters weaving figure eights just above her head. How glorious her sisters all are!

Ariel swoops down, mere inches away from Wendy, laughing as she passes. Wendy's hair whisks from the sudden rush of air.

"Fly, sister! Fly!"

Oh, how Wendy wishes to be amongst them. Soaring with her sisters!

Can she?

Wendy flexes her wings. There is a strain at her back. She feels like a toddler taking her first unsteady step. *How am I supposed to fly? Impossible. Absolutely impossible!*

Wendy glances over her shoulder, studying her own wings from the corner of her eye. Two separate sets—forewings at her upper back, hindwings below. They consist of a chitinous membrane. Hundreds upon thousands—perhaps *millions*—of tiny brilliantly shimmering scales. The thinnest filaments, colorful hairs, hold them together, forming a pattern. Yellow and black stripes with blue tears, an eastern tiger swallowtail, laced with dark veins.

"Move, wings," she orders. "I said move!"

The colors fluctuate the faster her wings flex, the tint like living oil paints, swirling and shifting the harder they flap. Blue now orange now green.

"Faster! That's it! Faster now!"

Wendy keeps flexing, beating her wings, until the strangest thing occurs.

"Faster..."

She no longer feels the ground beneath her.

"Faster..."

Wendy glances down and gives a gasp.

"My feet!" They are no longer touching the earth, inches off the ground! Look at her, rising into the air! Unsteady, yes, but buoyant.

"I'm flying! I'm flying!"

Just as quickly as the sensation sweeps over, gasping at her shallow ascension, her wings falter. "Oh—oh my—"

Wendy stumbles. There are only five or six inches between her feet and the soil, but still, the descent feels endless. Her heels promptly plop back onto earth.

Her sisters giggle.

No matter. Wendy is determined now. She pinches her face, taking a deep breath. Concentrating with all her might, she flexes her wings even harder.

"I will fly. I will fly. I will—"

Her ankles tilt. The tips of her toes leave the earth behind. One inch becomes two, then ten, until there is an arm's length between her and the soil.

The petals seem to shrink as she rises.

"Higher. Higher now..."

Wendy laughs, a walloping holler. She wants to go higher.

"Higher!"

The ground only grows smaller. Each flower blossom continues to constrict in a blink. The world is below and Wendy is above, soaring over it all.

"I'm flying," she shouts. "I'm—"

Something gives out. Her wings freeze, halting in mid-flap. Gravity greedily grabs at her feet and yanks hard, sending her plummeting toward the earth.

Wendy shrieks.

The wind hisses as she falls, a serpent in her ear, its darting tongue lapping at the lobe. The flower blossoms expand, growing fast now, quicker, the petals looking like a thousand gaping mouths opening wider, so hungry, ready to bite.

Just as Wendy is about to hit the ground—

She halts in mid-fall. Then flies, upside down. The world is all topsy turvy. Her hair falls into her face, blinding her. She has to blow her bangs away to spot—

Pippi!

"I've got you, sister," she says. The two soar into the air, together, Pippi's wings flapping steady and strenuous. "Don't be afraid!"

Wendy wraps her arms around Pippi, feeling her muscles flex, the firm root of her wings tensing at her back. What a beautiful, magnificent creature she is. She never wants to let go of her sibling. The strength of her. The beauty.

"Fly, sister," Pippi whispers in Wendy's ear.

Then releases her.

Wendy gasps but doesn't scream. The air feels like water, an ocean with no bottom. She falls, plummeting further by the second, the very breath, harder now, shriller, but she is determined not to hit the ground. She will not fall.

"Fly. I will fly."

Wendy flaps her wings. Harder this time. Her body is a boat, and her wings are the sail. She simply needs to find the right current of air, catch it, and fly.

"I will fly, I will fly."

The ground closes in. Her body slips into a spin, but she won't give up.

"I will fly."

And then... her descent diminishes. Those flowers below hesitate, no longer growing, shrinking in their circumference as Wendy lifts herself higher.

Wendy is soaring!

Sisters sweeps past, swirling around her as mermaids glide through water.

"You're flying, sister!" And she is! Wendy focuses on her wings, harnessing her own strength, and steering the very vessel of her self through the sky.

She shouts, "Woohoo!" Her sisters shout back, "WOOHOO!"

Watch them go. Sisters gliding through the air, laughing together. Watch them rise and drift and spin and spiral, playing like children. They soar for miles, glancing at the landscape below as it shifts in pigments. Endless fields of snapdragons and daffodils frantically lash in their wake.

Colors bend and bleed here, so close to the sun, the horizon a canvas of watercolors. There is no limit, no barrier that can contain these girls.

Up here, in the air, the sky red all around them, they are free.

"I'm free!"

How happy Wendy is, to be reunited with her lost siblings, at long last...

Just as God intended.

artist biography

There are times when he'll flip through his photo album in hopes of finding himself.

Even he doesn't recognize himself in the pictures, the beaming boy kept sealed behind a pane of cellophane, yellowing along with the remnants of Winston's childhood. The scrapbook is all that's left of his earliest years, a black and white testament to his life.

Who is that child?

That's not our Winston, is it?

I do believe so . . .

Look at Winston as a baby. Look at that newborn smile. Eyes so wide. The world has yet to consume him, frighten him with its shadows.

He reminds me of my son.

Son?

I had a boy his age. Long ago. Look at him . . . I remember those eyes. That smile.

You sound like you're sympathizing with him.

No, it's just . . . seeing Winston like this brings me back. I haven't seen my son in so long . . . My boy. He had hair like that, too. Cornsilk.

That's not your child. That's the face of your murderer—don't forget it.

Look at Little Winston getting baptized, blessed by the priest, water dribbling down his fontanelle as he wails away in his mother's arms, his father not so far behind, all smiles as their son is embraced by the loving grace of Jesus Christ.

Look at Winston in his Sunday best. No older than five. *Or six.* The suit itches around his collar, the boy scratching at his neck, his fingertip digging into the crevasse at his throat, eyes pinched ever-so as the shutter snaps and his image is captured, wincing into oblivion.

Where does the darkness begin?

When does he find the light?

Winston will drift through the pages of his scrapbook at night, passing from one black and white photograph to another, studying the hallmarks of his face. Even back then, as a baby, then a toddler, a boy, he's there, that timid individual, lingering within the eyes. The fear. The winsome distance. There's a yearning to be elsewhere. Far away from here.

A *wandering imagination*, his teachers all called it. It wouldn't be long before there was a concern amongst his tutors that Winston wasn't hitting particular developmental hallmarks. His growing mind wasn't flourishing. He couldn't read at the level of his classmates. His writing was slipshod, the letters too loose, unable to be contained by the confining lines of his marble composition books.

Slow, they called him. Autistic. Retarded.

His classmates said much, much worse. *Goof. Spazz. Dimwit shit-for-brains.* The names shellacked around his sense of self, slowly sealing him off from the world in the protective shell of his imagination. He shielded himself within his mind, feeble as it was.

He was held back a grade. Then another.

His mother took the reins on his education. For a spell, at least. He had no formal education, never surpassing fourth-grade level math.

Fifth.

No, it was fourth grade.

Fifth. Fifth grade. They had him learning multiples in mathematics, which is certainly something they save until they're in fifth.

I learned multiples in fourth grade.

It was Ms. Reynolds who tried teaching him.

Ms. Reynolds was his third-grade teacher. Ms. Leland was in fifth.

Oh . . . You're right. Ms. Leland taught him his multiplication.

Not that she got very far.

Winston's sense of history was snipped from picture books, blending battles into a morass of *Life* magazine photographs. But within that tortoise shell of a mind, barricaded beneath years of jeers and taunts, there will still be Winston's imagination, thriving, blossoming, a world unto itself.

This is where Winston lives. *In his own world.* With his muses, his true companions.

You'll always have us, Winston . . . No matter where you go.

Always and forever.

Can he hear us?

What is he thinking about now? What could possibly be on Winston's mind?

Shall we take a peek?

The stories his father brought home from the war found their way into his son. While there was still time between them, what Little Winston remembered, there were butterflies.

"Do you want to hear a story, Winston?"

Before deploying, his father read Winston from the Little Golden Books. *Bambi* and *Poky the Little Puppy.* Winston remembers their shimmering gold spines more than the stories contained in their pages. The illustrations hovered around the text, like clouds.

When Dad came home, he no longer wanted to read from those books.

He had other stories he wished to share.

"They made us walk for miles. If any of us fell down, the guards would shoot them."

Prisoner of war.

POW!

POW!

His mother muttered these words in passing to whatever friends or family came over in his dad's absence. Winston overheard them whispering, unsure of what they were discussing just out of his earshot. All Winston knew was that his father was away for a long, long time. Longer than anyone had anticipated. The waiting seemed endless for his mother.

When his father came back, he came back lean. His eyes had sunk into his sockets. His cheeks were barely held up by the bone below, sharp enough to cut through. His lips looked thinner than before, unable to cover his teeth anymore. Always sneering.

"There was no food for us. No water. *Nothing.*"

Winston was just a little boy, a child at the time, and yet, the images linger around the edges of his memory, pervasively invading his imagination. Stories of corpses decaying in trenches. Decapitated heads blinking back at his dad, as if they were still alive. Whispering to him. Telling his father stories that he brought back home to share.

"I had leather boots. I was lucky. Lucky leather. Anyone who wore rubber boots got frostbite. Lost their toes. Rubber doesn't absorb moisture like leather does."

Winston was far too young to remember much of his father before he left for Korea. A shame, really. There was love for his son. Winston himself might not remember it, but buried down deep in the back of his mind, there are the faintest impressions of bouncing on his dad's knee, giddily giggling, a baby on horseback, riding throughout the Western Plains. There are moments of taking flight, his father grabbing Winston's torso and spinning him through the air, the air sputtering out from his dad's lips like propeller blades humming.

Kisses on the forehead after drifting off to sleep. Tickles on the tummy.

Makes me sick.

Hush.

Well, it does . . . I don't want to think of him like this. See him like this. Do you?

What choice do we have?

Can we go back to the story now, please?

By all means . . . Have at it. Tell his story. Knock your goddamn socks off.

His father was enlisted at the age of twenty-eight, serving his country overseas for two endless years. Winston was only four when his father left. Perhaps younger. He was told by neighbors that he should be proud of his father, a hero, and in a way, he was.

POW. The letters were whispered all around Winston. *Pee-Oh-Double-You.*

What did it mean?

What came back home wasn't the same doting father from before. He was a shell of the man he had been before he'd enlisted. An empty vessel. He kept to himself whenever his wife was around, a mute in the corner of the room, staring out the window, waiting for an attack that always seemed imminent to him and no one else. His father waited until night, when Winston's mother was in bed, fast asleep, before visiting his son. To talk.

To tell his stories.

"They put me in a sweatbox. Ever heard of one of them? Couldn't have been any bigger than three feet high, two feet wide. Maybe five feet long. They squeeze you in. Cram you inside, no matter whether you fit or not. You understand that, Winston? It didn't matter if we fit. They'd stuff you in, seal you inside with a lid, then leave you there for days."

Stuff you in. Seal you inside. Leave you there.

Sound familiar?

"I couldn't move. Could barely breathe. I imagined I was a caterpillar. You know what I mean, Winston? I was a caterpillar in its cocoon, and soon, before long, I would hatch. I'd crawl out of there and . . . be something *different*. It was the only way to survive."

Every caterpillar must be frightened before it spins its own cocoon. How could they know what's waiting for them on the other side of that quiescence? How would they know the beauties that they will become? The longer Winston thought about it, rolling the notion over in his mind, the more it took root.

"I wanted to come home to you, son. I wanted to hatch out from there and fly home."

There were days when Little Winston would be left alone at home with his father, his mother at work, earning very little to support their family. "Someone has to put food on the table," she'd mutter before heading out, leaving the two of them together. Father and son.

It was then that Winston first learned about butterflies.

He found his father sitting at the edge of his bed, staring off at some vacant spot. The methodical metronome of a grandfather clock ticked away further down the hall.

Winston entered the room, head bowed, and coughed lightly. It was well past lunchtime and they had yet to eat. His father hadn't moved from bed.

"Would you like to see my butterfly collection, Winston?"

Little Winston nodded. Butterflies were beautiful. Butterflies were fun. He had no idea his father collected them.

Winston's father kneeled before their bed, leaning down and reaching under. He dragged out a trunk small enough to fit under the frame. A steel military case, padlocked.

Clink-clink went the brackets, unclasped.

Winston's father opened the trunk. A bittersweet tang of warm apples and mildew wafted out, filling Winston's throat. His mouth watered simply from the smell.

What's inside? The boy wondered, stomach grumbling.

A musty blanket the color of bruised avocados rested on top, folded neatly. Dad peeled it back, exposing a treasure trove of military memories. A bayonet knife, detached from its rifle. A deck of black and white photographs, held together by a rubber band.

A tobacco tin. On the lid, it read *Edgeworth Extra High Grade Sliced Pipe Tobacco. Larus & Bros. Co. Richmond, VA, U.S.A.*

"I've never shared this with anyone," Winston's father said, breathless, the tin resting in the palm of his hand. "I'm trusting you with this, Winston. Can I trust you, son?" The boy nodded.

"I had to hide it. Keep it close. I didn't want it to fly away . . ." His father carefully opened the lid, with a metallic pop, exposing a wad of cotton bandaging inside.

Winston held his breath as his father unraveled the bandage, slowly, gently, until a slope of flesh revealed itself.

An ear.

A severed human ear. The serrations along the lobe were crusted in dried blood. The skin itself had turned a deep purple.

"Beautiful, isn't it?" his father asked.

Winston felt compelled to agree, confused. When the boy slowly nodded, his father smiled. So proud of his son. Winston *saw*. The boy *understood*.

"My beautiful butterfly." He lifted his hand just a bit, above Winston's head, so he could no longer see the severed ear in the palm of his father's hand.

"Watch it take flight," his father said.

And so he did, following his father's hand. Away it went, flapping its wing.

Flying.

Winston's father hung himself two days later. Winston's mother was behind the makeup counter at Crinoline's when he wandered out the screen porch door, snapping shut behind him with that thin wooden *thwack*, traipsing through their backyard.

Winston waited for his father to come back, but he never did. The minutes ticked by and still he never returned. The boy's tummy grumbled, moaning low. Lunch came and went. Then dinner. When it got to be unbearable, he stepped out, following the same path as his father, to the woodshed behind their family's single-story clapboard house.

The door to the shed wouldn't shut, kicking open in the breeze and clanking. Winston took hold of the door, the color of elephant skin, its splintered texture in his hand, and peered in. His eyes were unaccustomed to the dark, slowly adjusting to its shadows.

There. Above the boy's head. Something majestic. An effigy swayed in the far corner. A hornet's nest in the shape of a man. A scarecrow dangling from the rafters.

What was it?

Winston's father hung by his belt, twirling. Every time his father's body turned, Winston could hear the strain in the belt, that stretching of leather. *Lucky leather.*

His skin turned a deep purple, a mottled hue, the capillaries burst in a bruised amethyst. His tongue pushed itself out from his lips, a final taunt, as if he were sticking it out at whoever found his body.

The purple skin. The protruding tongue. These are images that sear their way into this child's subconscious. Call it trauma, but we prefer to think of it as inspiration.

Colors yearning to find their canvas.

Winston went back inside their house, quiet as a mouse, leaving his father gently swaying in the midwinter breeze. Another secret to keep.

Can you imagine? What an awful thing to see . . . Especially for a child.

Yeah, how awful.

Do you think we'd be here now, if he hadn't seen his father like that? Do you think he'd be any different?

It was already in him, whatever it was.

I blame his mother.

Of course you would. The mother always gets blamed . . . Weren't we?

Not me. I was a loving mother.

I'll never know what I would've been. I never had the chance . . .

It's always the mother's fault. Always.

When Winston's mother returned from work that evening and asked where his father was, Winston never answered, lapsing into that catatonic spot where only boys hide.

His father's body remained there, dangling for days before anyone thought to look out back. To Winston, he was flying through the air, feet taking off from the woodshed floor.

He's flying still now.

Soaring.

Crinoline's was not a Macy's or a JC Penny's. This discount department store had branches cropping up across the Carolinas. The farthest shop up north was in Virginia, just outside of Richmond, less than thirty miles away from Brandywine, in a shopping center that would one day become the Cloverleaf Mall.

Winston's mother worked at Crinoline's for nearly seventeen years. Her coquettish smile served her well on thc salesfloor. When she was fresh-faced—beautiful, even—with emerald eyes and long lashes, she was tasked with working behind the makeup counter.

Women came in—mothers, mainly—and she would give them makeovers right there in the store. She was an *artiste*. These housewives—plain faces, porcelain flesh—were her canvas. She had a sturdy but gentle hand when it came to applying eyeliner and blush, turning these women into beautiful butterflies with fluttering long lashes and azure eyelids.

She considered it a craft. Her artwork lived within the frames of these women's skin. Stunning portraits of mothers and housewives. *These faces deserved to be hung in an art museum*, she would always say, tipsy. *Look at my masterpieces. I should be in the Louvre.*

Winston, only a child then, had no idea what a *Louvre* was.

He heard *lover*. Just said in a funny way. *Looover*.

As time wore on, the beauty Winston's mother once possessed began to fade. A particular spark diminished within her demeanor. She was unceremoniously relocated to the children's wear section. It felt like a demotion. A betrayal.

Where would she hang her masterpieces now?

There was always a glass in his mother's hand. Empty, then refilled. The liquid within burned Winston's nostrils. He slipped a sip once, after she'd fallen asleep on their couch.

That's not how it happened.

What do you mean?

You're getting the story all wrong. She gave it to him to drink.

No, she didn't . . .

She did! She was a bit tipsy, and she spotted Winston, looking all desperate, and she asked—Wanna sip?—*and the little boy nodded, so she gave it to him. End of story.*

That's not true . . . She would never do a thing like that.

Oh, is that so?

It tasted like kerosene, singeing his throat, setting a fire in his stomach. Winston never tried alcohol again after that. Despised it. His mother scorched herself from the inside out, night after night. Immolating her intestines with gin.

Wouldn't you?

I wonder if she knew . . . What her son was. If she sensed it, somehow, even then.

A mother always knows.

And still loves. Loves their child no matter what.

Of course they do.

If there was a sliver of silver lining to her new position at Crinoline's, it was this: Winston's mother now came home with clothes deemed unfit to sell. Torn hems or missing buttons, who could tell? Their manager told them to toss it. These defective items could easily be fixed, easy as pie, just as long as someone was willing to do the stitchwork.

Why not bring these clothes home? She sold defective childrenswear to all the other mothers in the neighborhood, cheap. Who else was going to put food on the table?

"Pinch them pennies," she would say to Winston, nipping his thigh with her fingers.

Winston would frown, shrink.

"What? You don't like it when I pinch your pennies, Winston?" She'd nip him in the thigh again. And again. "*Pinch* them pennies, Winston! *Pinch, pinch!*"

Winston's mother took her needle and thread and repaired these perfectly fine outfits. What she couldn't sell she gave to her son. Most clothes were for girls, but that didn't matter. Not at Winston's age. He couldn't tell the difference. Besides, free was free.

"Beggars can't be choosers," Mom muttered. "Certainly not in this goddamn house."

Winston's mother would not beg, much too prideful for that. "I never asked for a goddamn handout a day in my life, I'm definitely not starting now. You hear me, Winston?"

Even after her husband abandoned her and their son, taking the easy way out and taking his life, she never begged. "Leaving us to fend for ourselves," she'd mutter as she sewed, needles in her mouth, the pins in her lips, tips wriggling as she minced her words.

"What kind of man does a thing like that? Answer me, Winston. *What kind of man?*"

Winston never knew the right answer. He was never quite sure what his mother expected him to say, if she wanted him to speak at all. "Everyone calls him a hero," she kept at it. "Would a *hero* do this to his family? Would a real hero abandon his *wife*? Answer me."

One time he answered back—*He was a prisoner of war,* he mumbled—only for his mother to pluck one of the pins out from between her lips and prick his thigh. Just a jab.

He hissed. A bead of blood welled up from his khakis.

"Quit your crying," she said. "Hold still next time."

He tried holding still. Tried so hard.

He tried to keep quiet.

Tried.

When the tears were too much, Winston's mother pinched his lower jaw in her hand and squeezed, squeezed so hard his lips parted in her fingers, much like the rind on a crushed orange, opening his mouth.

"Children are meant to be seen," she said, scissors raised. "Not heard."

To prove her point, she opened the shears.

"One cut, Winston," she said, "and no one would ever hear you again."

Winston kept his mouth shut after that, learning his lesson, *speak only when spoken to, children are meant to be seen, not heard, quit your crying,* while his mind continued to spin. There were other places he could be, far-off worlds his imagination might take him.

Fly away, little butterfly . . .

Winston never waited long before he was miles away

from home. From his mother. She brought home old catalogues from previous seasons to show the other parents what she could offer them. Pictures of children giggling. Their laughter filled the house.

Winston flipped through. He found children in posed portraits from far-off places. Places he dreamed of being. Sledding through phony snow. At the beach. At school.

Anywhere but here. In this house.

See? What did I say? It's always the mother who gets blamed.

Here we go again . . .

Well, it's true—isn't it? Always gets the blame. I had left my husband after one too many black eyes; I'd broken my wrist after he threw me against their stove, slamming it down on the oven door to stop my fall, it was just an accident but the nurse on call asked if I needed help; I had never known how to ask for such things, where could I go, who would help me after years of internal bleeding and hidden bruises, breath held, heart pounding, so I told the nurse yes yes please help me *and I stayed at a group home for a month until my husband found me at the grocery store where I was picking up shifts and he begged me to take him back,* come home come home please baby, *and I took pity on him, I came home, and it wasn't long before the bruises came back blacker than before, deeper than before, a sprawl of angry storm clouds purple black and egg yolk yellow rimmed with burst capillaries, so when I ran away the second time there was no plan, no nurse to help, no group home, no path to guide me along or get me back on my feet again, I was just running, running for my life with nowhere to go, nowhere to hide, but there it was, the church, the church with its light on,* oh thank God *I said, actually said out loud, the answer to my prayers, maybe, just maybe there was someone here who could help me and* he *did.*

Well, now . . . How long have you been holding all that in?

Sorry . . . I'm sorry.

Don't apologize. Never apologize. We need to hold on to our stories. Don't forget.

We are, though, aren't we? Forgetting? Fading? What's going to happen to us?

Only time will tell.

No—not time. Winston. Only Winston tells.

In order to repair particular outfits, it became necessary for Winston to wear the outfit while his mother mended it. That meant slipping into these clothes. Girls' clothes.

"Don't budge, Winston," his mother would say, the diesel stench of her breath stinging his eyes. "Keep very, *very* still. I don't want to cut anything off by accident."

She always used her seamstress shears, bringing the blades up to his pelvis and—

snip snip

—cutting the frayed threads. Winston would hold his breath in those moments, terrified of budging, even to breathe, for fear his mother's shears would slice his skin.

She was so close to him when she worked. The proximity of their bodies was much too much. Her breath burned his eyes, the very reek of it leaving him queasy.

"What?" she'd ask. "What's wrong, honey?"

Sometimes she would slur her words, brandishing those blades in the air and—

snip snip

—tease him by cutting so close to his body. "What's the matter, huh?" Picking particular parts of himself and slicing an inch or less away. "Cat got your tongue?"

Snip.

"Cat got your nose?"

Snip.

"Cat got your ear?"

The serrations along the lobe. The crust of dried blood. The purple skin.

Winston's arm lashed out, smacking the shears out of his mother's hand.

"What the hell was that for? You hit me!"

When her manager at Crinoline's found out that she was reselling damaged items, she was unceremoniously dismissed. No forewarning, no severance. Just cut loose.

Snip.

His mother came home in a rage. Her breath smelled worse than usual, if such a thing were possible. "How do they expect us to *live*, Winston? How do they expect *me* to take care of *you*? How do they expect us to *eat*? With what *money*? *What*, Winston?"

Winston's mother drank without eating, without feeding her son. It became necessary for the boy to find his own food. He would rummage through the garbage bins of their neighbors at night, in the dark, a possum, which only got them talking.

When word found its way back to Winston's mother, she took it out on him. Found new ways to frighten him. Always with the scissors, brandishing those blades.

"I didn't raise a raccoon. Going through garbage. What are you? A *rat*? Eating *trash*?"

Winston huddled into himself on the floor, curled up in a ball. Crying.

"You playing possum? Is that it?"

She kicked him. Lightly.

"Answer me, Winston!" She leaned forward, snipping at the air at either side of his head—*snip*—at his left ear—*snip*—at his right, again and again—*snip, snip, snip.*

"What? Can't hear me? You got something in your—"

She only cut him that once. An honest accident. It was only the lower lobe of his left ear, anyhow. Barely a centimeter. Just enough to bleed.

She kept the bit of his ear in a mason jar. That tender fleck of flesh, burning pink, covered in blood. Why? Guilt, perhaps. How could she bring herself to throw away this tiny piece of her son? Winston's mother stored the mason jar in the pantry cabinet along with what remained of their seasonings. The pickled beets and preserved peaches.

She apologized profusely. Swearing she'd sober up.

Perhaps she did. For a while.

Now you sound like you're sympathizing with him, too . . .

I'm just telling his story. Isn't that what we're doing here? As biographers of the boy?

. . .Who will one day become a monster.

He's already a monster.

Still. It's his story.

Do you think that makes it okay? What he did? To us?

I never said it did.

What about us? Who's sympathizing with us? For you or me or her or her or—

What else is there? His story is all we have.

Everything was better before you came along . . .

What's that supposed to mean?

We had a rhythm. A routine. Then you joined and just had to start rocking the boat . . .

So, this is all my fault?

I'm just saying . . .

Where's the outcry over us? Where's our heartache? We get nothing.

No. We don't. Why not?

Because . . .

Because . . . what? What?

Because Winston's all we have. He's the only one who listens to us.

We're the only ones who can tell his story.

That's because we're the only ones in his head.

Is that what we are? I thought we were ghosts.

What else could we be?

Well, I want out of his story.

How?

I . . . I don't know. But I can't keep haunting him forever.

Forever's an awfully long time, isn't it?

If Winston ever had their home to himself, or his mother was passed out in the other room, he would make his way into the pantry, sealing himself inside those slat doors.

He would lift himself onto his tippy-toes, reaching for the top shelf. He could just barely reach it, blindly rummaging around the jars, terrified one might slip, fall, and shatter.

There. There it was. His fingertips felt the impressions in the glass.

He took down the jar. He twisted the aluminum seal with a tiny pop—*Plip!*

He carefully opened the lid, as if what was hiding inside might fly away.

A pink firefly.

The tip of his ear had shriveled. It looked like a scab now, salmon pink. Whatever blood remained flaked along the glass basin of the jar.

You would hardly notice the difference between his ears now. One is slightly shorter than the other, yes, but nobody minded. Winston himself had almost forgot.

Almost. We'll never let you forget, Winston . . .

Never ever.

I can't take it anymore. I need to get out of here.

Good luck with that.

His scissors are missing. He can't find his mother's shears anywhere. They are not where they're supposed to be, sheathed in their special leather holster on the folding metal tray table where he eats his meals. Where did they go? His shears can't just walk away.

The panic begins to simmer. Has someone been here? Inside his apartment? His studio? Rummaging through his stuff? Did someone steal his shears?

Winston tears through the space, searching everywhere for them. Everything in this space has its own particular place. Nothing ever disappears like that. Unless . . .

Would the Calverts have crept into his apartment when he wasn't around? Have they been in here before? They have, haven't they? What else have they stolen from—

Winston hesitates. He is kneeling next to his bed when he notices a glint from below.

There they are.

His shears are tucked under his bedframe, in the shadows, hiding from him. How in the world did they find their way under here? Winston wonders. Under his bed of all places?

We'll never tell, Winston . . .

A MOST DREADFUL ENCOUNTER:

In Which Our Dear Sweet Wendy Is Beset By The Wallowing Horrors Of War That Await Them All In The Muck And Mire...

Pippi turns, her breath caught in her chest. Her attention locks on a far-off spot. The others soon follow, their eyes sliding over the horizon.

The landscape shifts. What was a vibrant meadow moments before recedes into ruddy mud. Every blade of grass sinks into the earth, gone in a blink, leaving behind the craggy mire of an open field. All green is gone. What's left is red clay.

Blood.

"They're coming," Pippi says, breathless.

"Who?"

"<u>Them</u>."

Wendy doesn't see it at first. She can't quite understand what the others are so worried about.

The horizon darkens. The brilliant hues bruise themselves, an endless stretch of murky black and brown.

Out from the soil sprouts a winding twine of ivy which cuts through the turf, dragging up coils of thorned vines. There's a glint coming off from them, as if the tendrils are made of metal.

Those are no vines. No, not at all! So silver and sharp!

Barbed wire. The earth is rupturing in winding knots of steel teeth. A battlefield. Runnels carved into the mud. Red clay trenches.

What is happening here? Wendy wonders.

A sound catches in her ear, faint. A wet slopping. *Clomp, clomp*. Trapped air farts out from the pockets of mud, *burrap, burrrrap*, as if something is crawling her way. She can't see what it is yet, eyes racing over the mud.

There. Just ahead. What she sees crawling across the ground makes no sense to her. It's a man, that much is clear.

A soldier.

His ruddy fatigues feel oddly unfamiliar. He isn't dressed for any wars she knows. This soldier seems to be from some other era, completely outside her own.

His eyes are enormous. Massive circles the size of saucers. There's a glint within, light flashing off their glazed over panes, blinding Wendy. She can't help but wince. He looks like a bug. A praying mantis slinking around the muck.

Wait. Those aren't his eyes. *Glass*. Windows embedded into his sockets.

Not his face at all, then. No... It's a *mask*. This soldier's face is hidden behind canvas. The fabric is a drab olive green, clinging to this man's skin. Glass eyes, round and wide. The circled panes reflect the last of the sun, eclipsing this man's sockets. A proboscis curls and drags across the mud in front of him.

A gas mask. So *that's* what he's wearing!

That's a cylindrical screw-in filter canister. It has an accordion-like tube that toggles out from the base of the mask's mouth, containing activated charcoal to absorb mustard gas.

There is a raspy drag to his breath. Gravel at the back of his throat, raking across his windpipe. The air settles in the sack of his raw lungs and sloshes around.

"What on earth is that horrendous thing?" Wendy hears herself ask.

"Enlisted Netherman," Aurora says. "A swarthy soldier conscripted to serve the darker armies."

The wheezing man keeps crawling closer, closer, slithering over the battlefield like some primordial reptile, easing up from the ooze and shimmying on its fledgling limbs. It hisses and spits, its filtered gills singed from mustard gas.

"What am I supposed to do?"

"Stop him," Bambi says.

"Kill him," Pippi suggests.

"Crush him under your heel," Gretel adds lastly, with just the right amount of relish in her voice.

A bayoneted rifle is slung over the soldier's back, a serrated horn sawing at the fog. It slinks over his shoulders with every inch forward, jabbing at nothing.

The knife looks like the halved blade of a pair of seamstress shears.

I've seen those blades before, haven't I? Wendy wonders. *Those scissors feel awfully familiar to me... I know I have, but where?*

Wendy steps to the left, but Aurora grips her arm. "Don't run. More will follow. Always more. They hide the battlefield, rutting in the mud like fat piggies."

"You'll never see where they're hiding until it's too late," Gretel adds.

"You'll step right on one of them and"—Pippi claps her hands, summoning thunder between her palms—"they'll grab you, drag you under the muck."

At that, the soldier's crawl halts. He lifts his head, as if to sniff at the air.

He senses her. Smells the freshness on Wendy. The fear. The soldier's mask hisses with trapped breath, nearly squealing with glee. There's something so craven to his crawling, picking up his salamander stride, sliding over his belly.

"Oh my!"

It happens so fast. The soldier reaches her feet within a matter of a few giddy shimmies, grabbing fistfuls of clay and heaving his torso forward. Once there's no distance between them, the soldier takes hold of her bare legs. His fingers slip across her skin, the wet clay keeping him from getting a firm grip.

He's got her. He won't let go. His breathing seeps out from his mask, leaking air in an asthmatic rasp that nearly sounds like a laugh—hyugh, hyugh.

Wendy falls backward, screaming as she goes, landing on the earth with a wet slap. The rear of her summer dress is battered in ruddy mud, eclipsing its floral print.

None of her sisters rush to her aid. They remain where they stand. Watching. No—observing. This is a lesson learned the hard way.

"What do I do, what do I do, what do I—"

"Don't be afraid, sister," Gretel says.

Now that Wendy is on the ground, legs sprawled out, knees bent, the salamander soldier easily finds his way on top of her. His torso presses against her legs, sending them fanning out, a butterfly ready to be pressed and pinned in place, while he slithers further up, finally pressing his chest against her waist.

"Help me," she cries.

No one does.

Now Wendy can see his delirious eyes behind those panes of glass, so wide, hungry for her, bloodshot and chemical blue, staring down with the weight of battle and madness and desire that all men feel in the presence of something so young, something so beautiful, something to be possessed.

Hyugh, hyugh, hyugh...

His breathing intensifies, frantic now, seeping out from every possible crevasse within his mask, hissing like air escaping a punctured tire. Wendy feels the wisp of it against her own skin, hot and fecund, a man's decrepit breath, cigarettes and beans. No amount of activated charcoal can keep the smell of intestinal rot from reaching her, seizing her sinuses and flooding her mouth.

Hyugh, hyugh, hyugh...

"Stop! Please!"

The salamander soldier struggles to pin Wendy's wrists down. He takes his left hand to hold down her right, gripping her wrist and pressing it into the mud.

Hyugh, hyugh, hyugh...

"Let me go!"

Her left hand is still free. She swats his hand away as he attempts to grab it. All she has is her one limb, one hand to batter his chest, his shoulders, his—

Face. His face, hidden behind that canvas mask. A second skin of burlap. Those glass eyes, delirious headlights burning bright, cutting through the dark.

Hyugh, hyugh, hyugh, hyugh...

"I said—let—me—go!"

Wendy takes her free hand and grabs hold of the dangling charcoal canister. The accordioned hose collapses under her grip. She yanks the crenulated rubber tube with such force, it tears, much like uprooting a weed.

Hyuuugh—

The mask peels from the soldier's face. A sickening rip of skin fills the air well before the man begins to howl. How long has he been wearing this? Long enough to solder itself to his cheeks. What she sees underneath is red and welting, blisters and lesions. She has pried a scab too early, the wound below still fresh, still bleeding. The mask had somehow adhered itself to his face.

No, the gas mask *was* his face. A second skin. A fatty padding of yellow tissue below is now exposed, the sinew an angry red, steaming within the air.

Wendy flings the gas mask as far as he can, watching the hose spiral through the air, the panes of glass, now empty of their eyes, nothing but holes now, burnt bulbs. It lands further off in the battlefield with a sopping *splck*!

The soldier rolls off her, clutching his exposed face, the raw flesh blistering and bubbling in the open air. His howls are far more pronounced now, no longer barricaded behind the confines of his gas mask, free to shriek.

A man. He's just a man. Cornsilk hair, faded white. His rifle lies splayed in the mud, sinking below the surface. Wendy grabs it, plucking the weapon out from the mud.

She holds it up in the air, admiring the seamstress shears.

She runs her hand up the bayonet, using her thumb and forefinger to wipe the mud from the blade, exposing the metal—the glint of it, capturing that watercolor sun—before plunging it deep into the soldier's stomach, dragging it as far up as his chest as she can rake, the blade only halting on its path when it bumps against the lowest rung of the man's ribcage, arresting its ascension.

"Are you playing possum?" Wendy hisses. "Is that it?"

When she pulls the blade back out, the bayonet plucks a coil of the soldier's intestines, hot and steaming, a festive garland to this celebration.

Wendy rests the bayonet against the soldier's chest, his dangling organs still dripping, the faintest pitter-pat of blood smacking the ground below.

The girls tighten their circle around him, watching on as his breath turns shallow, then eventually stops.

"Marvelous work," Pippi says. "We'll make a soldier out of you yet, sister!"

artistic process

We hear his prayers.

Winston attends services twice a day. Some mornings, he's the only one in the pews. Turnout is so low these days: a devastating trend that's left Shiloh cutting corners.

I was never much of a churchgoer . . .

I was. Every week.

Look where it got you.

Stop it. Both of you.

Do you think he can hear us? Is he listening?

Who? God?

No, silly—Winston!

What God would ever ordain such a fate to befall His lambs isn't for us to say, but it was our fate. We came to Him in our time of need and, in his stead, he sent Winston.

What God, indeed.

Pastor Nat can always count on Winston fidgeting in the rear pew, hanging off every word as he plucks at the loose threads of his fraying coat.

Winston will even mumble the benediction under his breath, having heard the sermon so many times before he could lead it himself, if he were so inclined.

Night after night, we hear his whispered invocations fill the cramped confines of his carport apartment. It's not until his bedside lamp is turned off and the room slips into shadows that the beseeching begins, drifting across the darkness like a low hanging fog.

Winston begs for God to listen. Hear his call.

He huddles under the covers, a frightened little boy, pleading for his lord and savior to release him. This story, this epic tale he's been tasked to tell . . . it simply won't let him go. The story must be told, and he is its chosen teller. But look at what it's done to him . . .

Look how frail he is. How small.

How could I have fallen prey to . . . that. Him.

We all did, didn't we?

A story as momentous as this will inevitably take its toll on the teller. Winston won't survive its recounting. Already he's feeling the effects on his body, how it drains him.

So he prays for it to end.

His hushed litany is low and steady, the Lord's Prayer on a never-ending loop, a string of words that has no end and no beginning—*Our Father who art in heaven hallowed be thy name thy kingdom come thy will be done on earth as it is in heaven—*

Amen.

The words fade. Dissipate. The prayer's hold over Winston relents, dispelling itself, until the tight bundle of his body relaxes, every muscle ebbing its grip over his bones.

Asleep.

Even after Winston drifts off, the room slipping into silence, we hear his prayer. It has been spoken so many times in this suffocating space, the very words have soaked into the walls. Absorbed, somehow. His prayer will continue in this room long after he's gone.

So will we.

Winston . . .

Our voices, faint, follow him into his sleep. We find him. Drag him back.

Winston . . .

He wakes with a start, gasping for air, believing he's not alone.

He's not. He's never been.

We are here, always near, with him. Winston hears us wherever he goes.

Winston . . .

At first, he pushes away. He's imagining things. Making it up. But our persistent whispers prove he's not, always calling when he least expects it. What a fun game to play.

Do it again.

Winston lays back down, head settling into his pillow. He stares at the wall for an endless breath, waiting, listening, before giving up and closing his eyes. Let sleep take him.

Just before he drifts off . . .

Winston . . .

Winston bolts upright again, eyes wide. "Who's there?"

It worked! It worked!

He heard us!

Do it again! Again!

Oh, Winston dear . . .

"Leave me alone!"

If only such a thing were possible. Believe us, we would love nothing more in this world than to abandon Winston Kemper once and for all, rid ourselves from his existence.

Erase ourselves.

But fate binds us together, like the pages in a book. We are forced to tell his story.

He's not alone. Never alone.

He has us.

Winston . . .

"What do you want?"

Winston . . .

"Stop!"

Winston . . .

Pastor Nat, Shiloh's youth ministry leader, catches Winston hovering above the children during Sunday school. Winston prefers the sermons for the younger parishioners over the services for their parents. All the boys and girls have been ushered out from the main nave and escorted into a small classroom, the newly refurbished backroom, Winston's former studio, where Pastor Nat guides the kids through their very own tailored Bible lesson.

"Would you like to join us, Winston?" Pastor Nat asks. It's meant as a jab, a harmless joke, but Winston nods, much to the youth minister's chagrin.

Winston takes his time to kneel down, the crick in his knees clicking as he slowly situates himself amongst the boys and girls, towering over the rest of their heads by a foot.

"Now." Pastor Nat clears his throat, grinning at the kids. "Where were we?"

Winston sits in rapt attention, listening to the lessons stemming directly from King James. Stories of Jesus's resurrection. Rising up from the dead. This fleshly shell is nothing more than a vessel for that effervescent soul. It's what Jesus became—what we all become in the next life, the realm beyond, where we leave our bodies behind—that strikes Winston. No matter how often he's heard these stories, they always resound as if he were listening to them unfold for the very first time. They ring true to his heart like the clamor of church bells.

"Our bodies shall be transformed," Pastor Nat closes his eyes as he explains, "where we will be made like Christ's own resurrected body."

Transformed. A metamorphosis. The words sink in, even more so for Winston than the intended audience. He sits in slack-jawed silence, breath held. Mind racing.

Resurrected in the next realm. The world beyond.

When the lesson is done for the day and Winston is meant to help usher the children back to their parents in the pews, he stays behind. Something's burning on his conscience, that much is clear. His head is bowed, unable to meet Pastor Nat's eyes.

"Something troubling you, Winston?"

He has so many questions. More than the poor pastor can answer, try as he might.

"Do we all hear a divine calling?" There's a neediness to the question. A sense of timid desperation. Pastor Nat can't help but lose his patience, eager to move along.

"We are all called to serve, Winston, in our own little way."

Winston won't budge, blocking Pastor Nat. "But what if I've been burdened by a greater task? One that God's given only me?" Nat doesn't seem to like the sound of this. The pride in it. The sense of high regard. Who is he to feel this way? Winston, the *janitor*? What could possibly be his higher calling?

"God has a plan for each and every one of us, Winston . . . I'm sure He sees the hard work you do here and He appreciates all your service."

Winston's eyes widen. Brighten. "You think He sees me? Really sees me?"

Pastor Nat places a hand on Winston's shoulder, as gentle as clasping a child. "Have you ever considered being saved, Winston?"

Winston is born again, baptized right here in the Piankatank River.

Shiloh Baptist schedules its riverside services on the very last Saturday of the month. It's an on-demand ceremony. Volunteers sign up. Folks meet in the church parking lot before the sun rises, packing into the activities van to shuttle everyone down to the closest boat ramp, less than five miles away. The Piankatank laps at their feet, still black from dawn. If they time this right, the morning sun will strike just as baptisms begin.

A new dawn, a new day. Reborn.

Winston wandered across Virginia for most of his adult life, homeless and without family, working odd jobs that cared less about proper paperwork. Menial jobs. Slave labor. Dishwasher. House painter. He cut his hands. He burnt himself. He roamed with nothing more than the clothes on his back and a couple of clippings from his Crinoline's catalogue. He drifted from group home to group home for years before finding his way to Brandywine.

Shiloh Baptist took him in. "Don't mind Winston," the former pastor explained to the new. "He comes with the building." A part of the package deal. Every fresh reverend inherits Winston when they take over. It's unclear when he actually arrived. Nobody knows anymore. He's always been here, a permanent fixture to the church, as much as its pews.

Now they're set to save him.

Good luck with that.

The summer session combines both June and July's participants, nine members, all told, including Winston. The mosquitoes are out, even at this hour, clouding around the congregation as they wait. Members swat at themselves along the riverbank. The humidity is thick this morning. Each participant wears the same aquamarine t-shirt with a rendering of Shiloh on its chest. Winston's is a few sizes too big. They ran out of mediums, so his shoulders are swallowed up by a large, a child playing dress-up in his parents' clothes.

Winston watches as each congregation member is baptized before him. He stands at the very end of the line, shifting his weight from one foot to the next. They each shuffle up to the river's edge, taking off their shoes before stepping in, still wearing their clothes, where Mr. Jenkins, Shiloh's senior pastor, takes them into his arms, like dancing the merengue, and dips them into the waters.

Winston holds his breath every time they go under, gasping along with them the second they break back through the surface. What will happen to him underwater?

Will he drown?

Even now, he keeps glancing over his shoulder, seeking an escape. Perhaps he can wander off and nobody would notice? Perhaps he can disappear, make himself invisible?

"Winston?" Pastor Jenkins beckons from the Piankatank, up to his waist in water.

Winston doesn't move. It takes the assistance of the musical director, Mrs. Elmore, to guide him along to the river's edge.

What world will he enter once he breaks through the river's surface? Born again, but where? What will the world look like afterwards?

What will he become? A butterfly himself? A moth with a mustache?

Will God still want him?

Winston takes his first step into the water and his mustache flattens itself.

"Oh, my," he says. His lungs lock from the cold, chest seizing. His grip tightens around Mrs. Elmore's hand as she escorts him into the river. The mud below swallows his feet.

Pastor Jenkins takes Winston by the arm. "You are born again, Winston," he says as he presses a wet palm against Winston's forehead, "through the enduring word of God."

Winston instinctively winces, tears streaming down his cheeks, shrinking back into his frail frame in hopes of avoiding some attack, only to feel the pressure mounting against his temple, his back forced over, bending at the waist like some stalk hit by a mighty wind.

"Wash away our sins," Pastor Jenkins says, sending Winston further back, toward the waters. Winston's whole body shudders. Such a frail thing. He's crying, racked with fear.

Good. Let him drown.

Hush now.

The water first taps the back of his head, then quickly rises over his ears. All sound is swallowed. The pressure mounts at his ear drums. Winston gasps at the last moment, just before slipping under the surface. He pinches his nose, fearful of water worming its way in.

How long is Winston underwater? Less than a second. Two, at most.

Not long enough.

Stop it.

He opens his eyes and what he sees confuses him. The world is a blur, but the colors . . . The colors bleed in a brackish brown and green. The cloudy water, stirred up by all the activity, has a palpable pulse to it. A fluctuation of watercolors. He feels himself let go.

His old self seeps out from his body. He lets the spirit in.

When Winston breaks through the surface, gasping for air, water sputtering out from his mustache, purified of any sin, born again, he feels transformed. Altered, somehow.

His own metamorphosis is complete.

Winston taught himself how to paint. How to write. How to craft his fantasy worlds. His technique was wholly his own, primitive but distinct, bursting with ideas and images.

He's always imbibed books. Always buried in a novel, barricaded behind its cover, as if to hide from others. His own protective shell. Folks at Shiloh hear him muttering under his breath, reciting whatever he's reading. Most assume he's merely talking to himself.

He's talking to us . . . Weren't you, Winston? Just now? In your apartment?

He's not going to answer you.

But he can hear us, yes?

Why don't you ask him?

Winston? Oh, Winstoooon . . . Can you hear me? Blink once, if you can.

Stop playing games.

He blinked! He blinked!

Be careful with your belongings. Winston might take off with them. The Lost and Found at Shiloh is his main source of apparel. If a congregation member leaves it behind by accident, a hat or pair of gloves or socks, even just *one* sock, it won't be long before he is wearing it.

This goes for books as well. Mainly children's stories. For every Sunday school book drive, where families donate their kids' gnawed-on picture books, Winston gets first dibs. He pilfers the boxes of illustrated provisions, taking them back to his apartment.

He deconstructs these coloring books, taking them apart, removing the staples from the cover, much like a tinkerer dismantling a perfectly fine watch for its parts.

Winston cuts each picture out from the book and carefully files it away. There are so many folders holding hundreds of clippings, each divvied into their own category.

Weather. People. Animals.

When it's time to draw a particular vista, he has all the elements at his disposal. It's merely a matter of sifting through the myriad of folders, each holding their own illustration.

Butcher paper is his preferred canvas.

A roll—eighteen inches tall, one hundred feet long—costs less than five dollars at the local supply store. The lady at the counter will sell it to Winston for three if he ever comes up short, such as his last visit. What's meant for wrapping brisket or smoked meats ends up being the perfect material for his frenetic sketches. These reams of brown paper offer the vastest expanse to render his epic tableaux without the worry of reaching the end.

Pssst, someone whispers in the aisle. Winston turns, glancing over his shoulder.

The shop is empty.

Over here, silly, a young girl's voice beckons. It's the Morton Salt Girl. She's on the shelf, surrounded by so many of her selves, dozens of girls parading through the pale rain with their parasols. *You're so close,* they all sing in unison. *The seventh sister is nearly here!*

"When?" Winston asks the salt cartons, his voice tired. "How much longer?"

Soon, they sing, a choir of containers. *She will arrive very, very soon!*

"I don't know if I can finish . . ."

Don't give up, Winston . . . Stay faithful! Remain steadfast! Their voices are so cacophonous, filling the entire aisle. Their cartons shimmer in rain, the granules showering down, like diamonds. A thunderstorm against his skull, pounding. *We believe in you!*

With his roll of butcher paper now home, Winston has a never-ending battlefield, where the horrors of war can unspool before him in an immersive panorama.

There is nowhere to present his work beyond the carport apartment. This is his gallery. His very own museum. Winston merely rolls these endless scrolls into themselves, some reaching ten feet. Others longer. They take up the entire wall, an expansive tapestry that covers all four corners of his cramped apartment, filling the space from every side.

Winston is inside his own paintings.

He inserts himself in the battlefield, alongside the Butterfly Girls. He joins them in their epic quest, fighting to defend these children from the oppressive regime.

He uses his own likeness, on occasion, for those soldiers on the field. His features will do.

"Don't run," he reads from his own manuscript, play-acting all the parts. "More will follow! There are always more! They hide on the battlefield, rutting in the mud like fat piggies!"

Winston pretends, a little boy playing army soldier, miming explosions and rifle fire.

P.O.W.! P.O.W.! P.O.W.!

He'll get winded, imagining himself battling alongside his butterflies. It takes the air out from his lungs, all seventy-odd years of him. Or is it eighty? Who can say how old he is?

Does Winston even know?

Do we?

When was the last time he celebrated his own birthday? Not since he was a child.

Poor Winston, with no one to play with.

Would you like us to bake you a cake, Winston? Put a candle on it?

We'll sing "Happy Birthday" to you, Winston . . . Would you like that?

Altogether, ladies . . .

Collage has become his mode of expression. Whenever someone tosses a magazine into the trash, Winston's there to retrieve it. He's scored dozens, if not hundreds, of abandoned church periodicals. *Christian Living. Modern Catholic. Viewpoints* magazine.

Sometimes, he stumbles upon *People* or *Reader's Digest.* Maybe even a *National Geographic.* Perhaps a men's magazine. Those unnerve him most of all. All the leering advertisements, stubbled faces and cleft chins, telling him to buy this brand of chewing gum, or smoke this type of cigarette. Drink this particular whiskey. Be a man.

Be a man, damn it. You can do it, Winston . . .

Stop taunting him like that.

What? We're just having a little fun here . . .

I don't find this fun. Not at all.

Oh, come on . . . Live a little.

Live.

Winston never tries these creature comforts from the advertisements. He simply wants the pictures. He cuts around the chewing gum and cigarettes and whiskey, settling for the smiles. The lips. The eyes. Whatever product is being sold disappears. What's left is the reaction, the pleasure. The product doesn't matter, not anymore, long gone, clipped away. All that remains are the smiles. The blissful lips.

Winston captures that happiness. Utilizes those joyous

emotions for his own artistic purposes. Appropriates them. Those expressions are transplanted—transported—to the battlefield. To endless planes of poppy flowers. Of vast plateaus of sky, limitless sky, the horizon reaching across brown butcher paper.

Shiloh has a photocopier in its administrative office. A clunky contraption, practically as old as Winston himself. It takes some time for the machine to warm up, but when it does, Winston duplicates pages torn from his Disney coloring books, Bambi and Ariel and whoever else, dozens of the same princess photocopied into infinity, her expression echoing for pages and pages. He'll enlarge a particular image, blowing it up to enormous, near life-size, proportions.

No one in the office ever catches on to the deficiency of printer toner. The sheer amount of copy paper they go through month after month surely should raise an eyebrow, but no one ever guesses it's Winston. He's innocent in their eyes. Worse. Incapable. *Feeble*. A doddering old dolt. What on earth would he need to photocopy?

Winston keeps a particular coloring book right next to his bed. *Nursery Rhymes for Children*. He found it at the church years ago, tossed in the Lost and Found. Only a few of its pages had been scribbled in, the rest left mercifully blank. Its pages are brittle by now, yellowed and crumbling to the touch, but Winston never parts with it, by far his favorite.

Inside its pages are a catalogue of rhymes from Winston's childhood. Each song is illustrated by an individual picture, left intentionally colorless for kids to fill in the lines.

Winston takes his tracing paper and places it over those faces. Little Bo Peep. Little Miss Muffet. John Jacob Jingleheimer Schmidt. Their expressions encapsulate so much emotion—wide eyes, beaming smiles, tearful cheeks—that he replicates, tracing every illustrated face in their flurry of feelings.

Winston is not a master craftsman. This is the sad truth. He doesn't possess the capacity to manifest any of these emotions from his own free hand. He needs someone else to do it for him. That's where his catalogue of images comes in handy. At his disposal is a treasure trove of emotions, ready to be replicated, depending on what his story calls for.

If he needs a sad face, he flips to the image from Little Bo Peep.

Look at those tears! That poor girl has lost her sheep! They'll never come home now!

Her tears become our tears. Her sobbing face becomes ours. The pinched eyes, the open mouth, crimped lips. From the hollow grotto on the page, out come our voices.

Look at us. Look at what we've become. Reduced to a children's illustration.

She looks nothing like me.

I don't even remember what I looked like anymore . . .

It's fading for me, too. I'm forgetting. We all are.

Not me.

Of course not you. You always remember everything, don't you?

I do! I remember everything! I was lost, which I thought wasn't possible what with phones and map apps and everything else that tethered people together, but here I was lost genuinely lost in the state of Virginia with no idea where I was or how close to the nearest gas station, and how does someone get themselves into a mess like this in this day and age; I just had to laugh, laugh at myself, what a complete frickin' moron, I couldn't find my way out of a wet paper bag, ha ha ha, oh well what was I gonna do but walk along the highway here until either a car passed me by and picked me up or I came across a house and asked to use their phone, but hello lo and behold what do we have here, the answer to all my prayers, ha ha ha, a church all the way out here in the middle of nowhere; well beggars can't be choosers, but it's a Tuesday, are churches even open on a Tuesday, let's see if anyone's around, hopefully someone will be there to let me use the phone and he *did.*

Winston always did, didn't he? For you and for me and for you and . . .

Always.

Whenever Winston needs to show one of his girls in terror, gasping as her guts are bayoneted before her own eyes, he flips to the page containing Little Miss Muffet.

There is no spider sitting down beside her. It's a soldier now.

The expression of fear remains the same, replicated over and over by Winston's unsteady hand, duplicating Little Miss Muffet's shock, now stripped of its original context.

The fear remains, even if the catalyst changes.

If Winston is hoping to show a look of love, of joy, well, look no further than Mary and her little lamb, always following her wherever Mary went, Mary went. Sometimes, Winston hums along to the song as he traces their new face, *Its fleece was white as snow . . .*

Look at how loving their expressions are. Look at the *joy.* The simplest hint of a grin.

Where's the lamb? Gone now. Winston doesn't need the animal anymore. All he wants is the girl's expression. Her love. The image will suffice.

He's a thief. A murderer and a thief. Aren't you, Winston?

You're goading him.

So what if I am? A thief, Winston. You're nothing but a thief of human beings. You take what you want and toss the rest . . .

Once he has picked the proper visage, extracted from the page by his own hand and captured on tracing paper, he takes her wherever he wants. Uses that expression however he wants. Their faces are no longer bound by the nursery rhyme they originated within.

These girls belong to Winston. He can redraw them in whatever situation he wishes, using any one of the countless faces he's traced over the years.

There is a particular clipping, snipped and filed away in the stacks of articles Winston has kept over the years, yellowed by now. It contains a photograph of a girl sticking her tongue out at the camera. It's a winter picture, that much we can tell. She's wearing earmuffs, this child. Her tongue reaches straight down, across her bottom lip, the tip at her chin. She's holding an icicle in her mittened hand. The caption along the bottom reads:

TOO COLD TO HOLD!

Where have I seen this tongue before?

We've seen it several times, a hundred times, replicated into infinity by now, popping up in Winston's massive panoramas.

It's our tongue. Ours now, at least.

Winston photocopied that girl's face, years ago, taking her tongue to trace in order to reconfigure it, repurpose that girl's expression for countless drawings he's done since.

He appropriated her tongue. Gave it to his girls.

How considerate. Thank you, Winston . . .

Yeah, thanks.

That tongue only comes out in his drawings of children being strangled. Whenever they're in pain, wounded on the battlefield, there's that tongue from the newspaper clipping. It's the same expression, repurposed and redone endlessly, displaying their pain.

Our pain.

Winston can't draw the expression himself. He always traced it. Pilfered the expression of others and repurposed them.

What other images comprise his girls? Where do they come from?

Who are we now?

He's done this for nearly every emotion. The very fragments of their bodies have been stolen. Now they are a stitchwork of different images, all patched together.

Then Winston sends his girls off to battle. His imagination has enlisted us to fight in his far-flung fantasies.

Winston sought out innocence. Sought to return our physical bodies—the women we were—back to some pure state of incorruptibility in his drawings.

To be reborn. Born again, transformed. A watercolored metamorphosis.

We were lost. We were destitute. Winston changes all that. He gives us back our innocence, reborn as butterflies, then mobilizes us to fight for him in his holy war.

If it's a war Winston wants, let's give him one . . .

Something shatters.

An explosion of glass wakes him and Winston bolts upright in bed, met with darkness. The only illumination comes from the motion detector light mounted to the back patio porch on the main house, its beam reaching through the window overlooking the driveway. The light spreads over the kitchenette wall, illuminating a pillar of catalogues.

Everything is still. Nothing moves throughout the space.

There is the faint bristle of leaves rustling outside the garage, a tree branch scratching at the walls, but nothing more.

Winston stands. He hesitates, listening. Straining to hear something, anything.

There's nothing. Nothing at all.

Did he dream it? It's quite possible. Perhaps it had just been his—

Winston . . .

There. From some far-off corner of the apartment, hidden behind the barricade of catalogues and notebooks . . . a sound.

What was that? A voice. His name, whispered from within the room.

Winston says nothing in return, holding his breath, standing very still and straining his ears, listening, listening, waiting for them to repeat themselves, whoever they may be.

Where are they hiding?

Breaths pass—and still, nothing. The motion detector light outside clicks off, plunging him back into blackness.

Could it have been the wind? The sound had been so faint, barely a breath.

His imagination, then. Just his fevered mind making him jump. Such a scaredy cat—

Winston . . .

There! There it is again! This time he's certain of it. Closer now. Whoever they are, they know his name. Taunting him, teasing from the shadows.

"Who's there?" The sound of his own voice is feeble. Ineffective. There's no threat to it. He can't hide the fact that he is afraid. It's there, in the very words. Not a demand; a plea.

No one answers.

Winston steps forward in the darkness, then takes another, navigating around the stacks of yellowing newspapers and crumbling coloring books, until he makes his way into the kitchenette. The shift in space is designated by the carpet ending and linoleum tiling taking over the floor. Whatever mess he might make is easier to scrub up that way.

The motion detector outside snaps back on, pouring light inside the apartment. Winston almost feels caught, freezing in the spotlight. Should he hold up his hands?

The cabinet door is open. *Odd.* Winston never leaves it open. The cabinet is always closed. The row of mason jars now glows from its shelf, capturing that obtrusive beam from the motion detector light pouring forth from the window, just behind his shoulder.

One of the jars is missing.

Six are now five. His most recent acquisition is no longer on the shelf. A space remains where the jar is meant to be, a child's lost tooth, that gap exposed for all to see.

Crnch.

Winston hears the crumble of glass underneath his bare foot before he even feels it. The pain takes longer to reach his nerve endings, the sound of it much stronger.

Glass. Broken glass. Shards digging into his heel.

Winston glances down and spies what remains of the mason jar, shattered along the floor. Toothsome bits curling up in crescent fangs. There's blood beading the linoleum.

Did I do that? I did, didn't I?

We all did. Together.

And what of our uvula? Whoever's jar this was, their mottled glass coffin, where is that plucked piece of fruit, all shriveled and dried? It must be around here somewhere . . .

Our voice is now free.

Winston . . .

The motion detector clicks off, abandoning poor Winston in darkness once more.

Oh, Winston . . .

Another mason jar slips, seemingly on its own. It tips off the cabinet shelf, plummeting to the kitchenette floor and shattering across the linoleum.

Winston . . . Can you hear us?

Another jar falls. A crystalline hand grenade. It even has the same mottled grip along its surface, the pin pulled, the countdown to its detonation beginning in three . . . two . . . one.

Winstoooooon . . .

Our voices are everywhere now, free from their glass prisons.

We want to have a word with you, Winston . . .

How about several?

Are you listening, Winston? Are you all ears?

THE HORRORS OF WAR:

Our Butterfly Girls Are Faced With The Atrocities Of War First-Hand... An Impassioned Speech Stirs The Girls' Hearts As They Ready For Battle...

Wendy can smell it. A lingering fetid stench, this cindered hint of burnt flesh drifting through the air. That acrid tang clings to the back of her throat, an oiliness coating the roof of her mouth.

Is there a fire nearby? There must be, she imagines. What's burning?

"Where are we going?" Wendy has to ask.

"Ssh," Pippi hushes her. "They'll hear you..."

Wendy bows her head, properly chastised. Children should be seen, not heard...

A somberness sweeps over the rest. Temperaments grow dense, much like the clotted air, thick with a mayonnaise of malaise.

Pippi takes pity on Wendy. She turns back to her sister and gives a comforting smile. Her lips fail to remain uplifted for long. "Prepare yourself."

Wendy doesn't like the sound of that one bit, no... "Are we in danger?"

"You'll see soon enough, silly," Ariel

answers. "We must save our sisters and battle against the Squareheads and their Expeditionary Forces..."

"We will be at our strongest when all seven sisters are united," Pippi says. "Then we'll be able to free the children of this world from their enslavement."

Squareheads? Expeditionary forces? What sort of war is this?

"*Ssh*," Pippi hisses, halting. "There they are!"

What Wendy sees takes her breath away.

Children. So many children, wearing their Sunday best. Pigtails and skirts. Back-to-school clothes. Fall fashions. Strung from the burnt trees, lynched little children, bound to the branches by barbed wire. Disemboweled boys and girls.

The fronts of their school clothes are drenched in watercolor red, blood distorting the lines that were meant to keep their colors contained.

A sausage string of intestines extends from tree to burnt tree, twined together in some grisly christening. Some children still wear their smiles, grins fashioned from images that contrast the horror unspooling from their bellies.

Standing amongst the trees are gas-masked soldiers. Their eyes remain hidden behind glass panes, reflecting the charcoal sun. A sibilant hiss dissipates from each mask, ventilating their breath with ragged gasps. Their bayoneted rifles are pressed against their chests as they march. Each has the halved blade of a seamstress shear fastened at its end, same as the last soldier. Dull copper.

With little remorse, these soldiers bring

the scissor blades of their bayonets up and snip off the lower lobe of each child's ear. Just a fleck.

"Cat got your ear?"

The children let out a cry, which makes the men all laugh before plunging their bayonets deep into their chests. Graphite tears stream down their cheeks.

"Oh," Wendy gasps. "Oh, my!"

The soldiers rummage through the guts of every girl and boy before bringing out their bowels, decorating the surrounding trees with the child's insides. "How horrifying," Wendy manages. "What monsters these men must be!"

"Now you see what horrid forces we are up against," Bambi says.

"How do we stop them?"

"With every ounce of strength we can muster," Gretel says.

"But there are so many of them, and so few of us!"

It's true. There are countless soldiers. Soldiers that make no sense. Confederate infantrymen from the Civil War intermingle with the Doughboys, Krauts and Nippons from the Great Patriotic War, Cossacks, and Green Beret grunts to form a motley battalion, chortling and singing songs of wars fought and won, the air scintillating with the stench of death, their fetid breath, madness and decay.

"This war has been waged for ages," Aurora shares. "They have come to our planet to enslave our children. Some are even..." She can't finish, bringing her hands to her face and shielding her eyes, the horror much too much for her.

Gretel finishes for her, all gruff. "Some children are <u>made an example of</u>."

Steel drums are set all around the

battlefield, FEMA stenciled across their broadsides, belching black smoke into the air. Each metal barrel holds a hideously roiling fire. The flames lift, flickering yellow tongues lapping at the sky.

Wendy watches as a Confederate takes the steaming entrails of a boy, picking them up by the end of his bayonet and plopping them into the drum, feeding the fire with a sibilant hiss. Hisss! Hissss! Hissssss! The flames greedily devour the entrails, the flames growing a russet umber.

"How do we fight them all?" Wendy can't hide the tremble of terror in her voice. "There are bound to be hundreds of soldiers! And only six of us!"

Aurora takes in a resolute breath. "Listen, sisters," she begins. "Today is the day we take back what has been taken from all of us. Our innocence!"

A breeze blows through, whipping up their spirits and bristling their bobs.

"Look upon today as the day we reclaim our honor," Aurora continues, chest held high. "It will be a day of blood, yes. There will be great loss... But when the smoke clears and we honor the fallen, we will look upon our victory and recognize that today—The Day of Reckoning, the Day of the Great Saving, the Reclaiming of Begotten Boys and Girls—was your birthright as a Butterfly Girl!"

Wendy feels a stirring in her chest. A whirlwind of adrenaline.

"Victory is in your throat, sisters," Aurora cries. "Let it roar! Shout for your siblings! Know that the tides of mankind shifted on this blissful battlefield!"

Yes! Wendy feels it, her very spirit stirring.

"Generations of Butterfly Girls will whisper our names, the names of the brave, the victorious! They shall always have our names in their hearts!"

The atmosphere fluctuates. Wendy feels the air stir, the beating of her sisters' wings whipping up wind all around, gaining speed, flapping faster now.

"Do not be afraid, sisters. You are not alone. You are all Butterfly Girls and you shall soar to the heavens to be embraced by those who have flown before you! You are the chosen soldiers, plucked by the very hands of God!"

Wendy feels that fluttering in her chest. A mighty stirring, gaining speed, a holy momentum, eager to be free. To fly.

"Our numbers may be small," Aurora calls. "But we are strong when we are united. Six—soon seven—sisters! A mighty alliance, at long last! We may be afraid, but together, we are fearless! Together, we are a mighty fist of innocence!"

The other girls feel it, too. This stirring. Their wings won't stay still, beating at the air, pounding the atmosphere into submission.

"Are you ready to fight, my sisters?"

"Yes!"

"Are you ready to free those pressed under the thumbs of men?"

"Yes!"

"Are you ready to take back what's been taken from us?"

"Yes, yes, yes!"

"Then let us spread our wings and fly into battle together! As one! For we are the Butterfly Girls and Butterfly Girls fly and fight together!"

"Fly and fight!" The girls all cry, Wendy loudest of all, releasing a howl that fills the charcoal sky.

"Chaaaarge!" And just like that, our six sisters, the Butterfly Girls, launch out from their hiding and take to the air, racing into the battlefield from above.

What a majestic sight they all make as they fly into battle! What beauty!

inspiration comes calling

At long last, Winston's prayers are answered!

The seventh muse finally comes calling. The end is near, finally. *Finally.* Winston can end his pilgrimage. The relief of it all. The downright unburdening. He feels it in his shoulders. The weight bearing down on his bones.

How long has he waited for this exact moment? How long has it been since the transformation of the sixth sister? Nearly a decade now? Perhaps more? The years are fading, blending together, even for him.

Do we even know how long it's been? How much time have we lost?

I can't remember.

Who was last?

You?

Me? I thought it was you . . .

Hold on. Try to hold on to ourselves.

I don't know how much longer I can . . .

Winter is nearly here, sapping the sunlight far sooner than before. Dusk is upon him, a crisp chill in the air, seeping into the nave as the light dims.

Winston has been repairing a step on Shiloh's side

entrance. The metal banister has come loose, the screws in need of tightening so elder congregants can keep their balance.

Just as he's wrapping up his work for the day, he senses electricity in the air.

Do you feel that? Something's different . . .

Particles gathering. Coagulating in the atmosphere.

She's here. Winston knows it. It's in his bones.

The seventh sister.

It's her . . .

Who?

Her. Another one.

Another . . .?

Oh. Oh no, no, no . . .

She's here. The seventh.

No. No, that can't be . . .

Winston gathers his tools. Steps inside the church. He wants to see her.

To finish this.

What do we do? What do we do?

Stop him.

How?

Think of something!

Who will Winston be without his stories? What will happen to him after he's finished? No matter now. There's work to be done. He must prepare his muse for her transformation. Her watercolor baptism. Her rusted chrysalis awaits out back. It's never a simple task. It takes so much energy. He can barely lift his arms over his head anymore.

Can he even complete God's mission? His divine calling?

No. Oh no. Look.

It's her.

Sure enough—there she is, nestled in the second pew.

Her black hair is an explosion of ink across the canvas of her pale face. She is a Rorschach test of radiance. She sits upright, her attention on the sanctuary, the chancel, the empty lectern, the altar itself.

Her name is unknown to him. He doesn't know her story. He prays he never does. Her life is a mystery to him until the moment she is absorbed into Winston's masterpiece.

No, no, no . . . We can't let him get away with this. Not her, not another.

We have to fight back . . .

We can't.

Yes, we can! We can't let him take her. Not like he did with the rest of us.

What do we do what do we do what do we do?

Fight! Fight back! Our numbers may be small, but we are strong when we are united! We may be afraid, but together, we are fearless! Together, we are a mighty fist!

Winston has to steady himself. His body has grown so fragile. He's trembling. Either out of nervous excitement or his years, he can't say. Perhaps a bit of both. His bones ache.

Can he even capture his muse anymore?

Look at him. Just a doddering old man. So wrinkled, so withered. Hair crops out from every canal. His mustache hides his mouth, filled with crumbs from long-forgotten meals. That unkempt mop on his head recedes over his liver-spotted scalp, a patchy terrain over his bare pate. Who could this man ever harm?

How can we fight back? How can we do anything? Winston never listens . . .

Maybe . . . maybe he will.

Maybe he'll what?

Listen.

To us?

The air around this woman is electric. See how she glows. Purples, blues and blacks. The atmosphere distorts all around her, blurring into watercolors. Such a vision.

Winston knows the time has come. The seventh sister! He can finish his gospels. The child slave rebellion will soon be over, and he will be released from his duties as scribe.

Winston never asked to be the chronicler of their story, much like we never asked to be participants within his tale, intertwining our lives within his Biblical mission.

This is the fate chosen for us all. Winston merely answered his calling, bestowed upon him by a higher power. The Morton Salt Girl, an angel, descended from the heavens.

He has been the bard of the butterflies for decades, and now, soon, it will all be over.

So close. The ending is so close, he can practically taste the words.

The end. What sweet words. So close, *the end*. Bleeding fruit. Plucked from their soft palates. *The End!* At long last! He just has to complete the tale.

One more muse to go. She has come calling. Time for Winston to answer.

Winston still has his toolset from fixing the banister. The screwdriver remains in his hand. He tightens his grip around the plastic handle, the crack of his knuckles nearly giving him away. The arthritis throbs through his hand. The pain is low and swelling, thick and persistent. A molasses in every knuckle. No matter. He's so close. No turning back now.

Maybe we can distract him. Get in his head. Flood his mind with our voices.

Do you think it'll work?

We have to try . . .

Winston makes his way down the aisle, careful not to draw attention to himself. He can't help but hear every creak within his own bones, cracking joints echoing throughout this holy space. It overwhelms his senses. The strain on his body, it's too much for him.

What a fragile old man he is.

Perhaps it's the dimness of the late afternoon, but this woman's body radiates blackened brushstrokes. They drift off her shoulders, these watercolors, bruising the air. She came here for solace, whoever she may be, that much Winston knows. Something has drawn her here. Her heartbeat is steady, a rhythm he can recall from all our chests.

It's Winston's own heart he should be concerned about. His pulse is erratic. He can hear its odd staccato rhythm in his chest, like a litter of kittens stuffed in a pillowcase.

We hear it, as well.

Squeeze it.

Rip it out.

Winston pushes on, determined now, even as dizziness clings to his thoughts.

The woman, she's so beautiful. So striking. Already he can see her wings unfurling from her shoulder blades. What color will they be? Adonis blue? Yellow? Green?

Will she be a dingy skipper? Pearl-bordered fritillary? Red admiral? Painted lady?

Soon. All these questions will be answered soon enough. Every gestation, every metamorphosis is a miracle. Into the steel cocoon these women go, undergoing a transformation within the confines of their own rice barrel, and when they finally emerge, what crawls out is a wondrous sight to behold. A miracle of the imagination. Of God's will.

These women are reborn, ready for battle. Their holy war awaits.

Hurry!

Do something! We are Butterfly Girls and Butterfly Girls fly and fight as one!

Now!

There will be a moment of pain, yes. Blood, perhaps. But when she wakes, she'll be one of us. Amongst her orphaned sisters. Enlisted in an endless battle.

We seven sisters have been separated for so long, too long, but now we will finally, *finally* be reunited and put an end to this war that has taken the lives of so many.

Winston is so close now. Any misspent breath will surely give him away. And yet, the woman hasn't budged. Hasn't sensed his approach. She's like a statue of the Virgin Mary, that beatific smile. That placid expression. She's at peace. She's ready to transform.

A pupa pining for her cocoon. Her steel drum awaits.

Winston will have to hurry, if he's to hide her body before daybreak. He'll have to empty the grain into the dumpster out back. Then stuff her body inside the barrel. He's kept count of the drums over the years, tallying the amount of cocoons he has left.

Only one barrel remains. His final egg sac.

Let's begin, he thinks to himself.

To us. Only we hear him.

And he can hear us . . .

Winston raises a trembling fist, the flathead reaching out from his hand like an antenna, quivering through the air. The muscles in his arm burn. He can barely lift his arm.

So close. *So close.*

He whimpers. Just a bit. He doesn't want to startle her, but he's shaking so much.

Winston . . .

The candle flames in the nave flicker under our breath. Some extinguish themselves under the gust of our collective exhale, drifting across the pews.

Winston's eyes widen. He grinds at his jaw, chewing his own tongue. He's flushed.

Winston . . .

He's certain he hears it. His heartbeat picks up, that shriveled engine puttering under such duress, sputtering along.

It's working! Keep it up!

Winston . . .

Louder!

Winston . . .

Where is it coming from? Where are they? Where—

"Hello," the woman says, startling poor Winston. He gives a start, looking as if he's about to jump out from his own skin. The liver spots on his scalp practically hop off, much like the leopard losing his own spots. Wasn't that a story Winston heard as a child? It was a fairy tale his father read to him before bed, before he was shipped off to war. Before coming back all broken. Before he brought back his butterfly collection, sharing it with Winston.

Oh, Winstoooooon . . .

The screwdriver slips from Winston's arthritic grip and falls to the floor. The plastic handle clatters across the tatty red carpeting in the center aisle and rolls under a pew.

"Sorry," this young woman apologizes. She brings her hand up to her mouth, blushing. What an awkward moment. She's embarrassed. "I didn't mean to frighten you . . ."

Her. Frightening *him*. How humiliating! Look how far he has fallen.

There are no words. He can't speak.

Cat got your tongue, Winston?

Meooow . . .

Hsssss . . .

The woman leans in closer. "Can I help . . .?"

Winston waves her off, muttering to himself as he kneels—joints straining, muscles pinching—the pop of sockets an elderly aria. Hear how his body sings, his bones a choir.

It's working! Keep it up! Keep it up!

Winston . . . Oh, Winston . . .

What's wrong, Winston?

His free hand grabs hold of the pew to support him on his wobbling descent, knees cracking as he bends, searching desperately for that flathead. Where did it go?

It must've rolled further away, underneath the next pew. He can't seem to find it.

Having trouble, Winston?

Where's your weapon?

There's still time, he reasons. The element of surprise may be gone, but no matter. He just needs to find the screwdriver. Where on earth did it roll off to?

That's it, keep looking, it's bound to be around here somewhere . . .

The young woman is still talking. Winston's attention drifted away from her. He has to catch up to the words, but all he can do is simply blink back. A dumb mute of a man.

"Hope that's alright?" She tries again. "The front door was open, so I figured . . ."

Winston is about to answer, to say something, but—

Winstooooon . . .

—the words are caught in his throat.

The young woman carefully picks herself up from the pew. She's wearing a drab green military jacket that's far too big for her. Where did this girl get it? The Lost and Found?

Just who is this woman? Nothing but a child, too young for war. Too—

Oh, Wiiiinston . . .

—innocent to have seen the horrors a jacket like this would suggest. She's drawing nearer now, reaching out to Winston. Offering her hand to him. There's a look of concern on her face. She's worried. About him. What a pitiful, miserable creature he must make!

So close. He's so close. It's not too late. If he can just find the flathead. He can still—

What's the matter, Winston?

—transform her. Can't he? There's still time, isn't there? He's too old. Too feeble for this work. He doesn't have the strength. His own bones and muscles are failing him.

You'll never get another, Winston . . .

"Are you alright?"

You're ours now, Winston . . .

"Is there someone I can call?" the woman asks.

Call us, Winston . . . We'll answer.

The muses surround him. Whisper into his ear. *Winston.* It's all he hears.

We're here . . .

Winston knows these voices. He knows whose mouths they came from. We are with him, always and forever. We are free from our mason jars, our glass prisons.

We will never let Winston go. Our voices linger in his mind, overwhelming every last thought, until there is nothing left to think, to hear, to know.

His muses will be heard. He must answer for his art.

Winston . . .

Winston . . .

Winston . . .

Winston stumbles back, collapsing onto the floor. He

crawls off, scrambling down the aisle, away from this young woman. She can only watch him, flabbergasted, unsure if she should help. But nothing can help Winston, not ever again, now that there is hell to pay.

That's it, Winston . . . Run . . . Run as fast as you can . . .

We'll find you, no matter where you go . . .

Run, Winston . . . See if you can hide from your muses now . . .

A DAY OF RECKONING:

The Day Of The Great Saving... The Reclaiming Of The Begotten Boys and Girls... The Grim Cost Of Victory... A Fallen Comrade Mourned...

Brilliantly blinding wings, such wondrous colors, soon eclipse the sun. The air is theirs, the sky their vantage point against these earth-bound armies.

"Dive!" Gretel shouts. "Dive! Dive!"

Gretel performs a perfect downward spiral, diving in a blinding corkscrew of color. The spots on her wings blur into rings of orange and black.

The rest follow, one sister after another, plunging in a divebomb formation.

Wendy is last, taking a deep breath before spinning, spinning, spinning...

How beautiful these brave girls are, soaring through the air!

What wondrous warriors!

The gas-masked soldiers lift their eyes. Their reactions remain hidden behind cataracted panes of fogged glass. They take their battle positions, raising their weapons, seamstress shears slicing at the air, cutting it open. Imagine a livid sea urchin, its tines writhing in every direction, jabbing at the atmosphere.

"Spare no one, girls," Aurora commands. "Release hell upon them all!"

Gretel grabs a man by his gas mask, wrapping her hand around the hose and yanking back, exposing the tender slope of his throat below. This affords Bambi a perfect opportunity to slice his slender neck with her antler, flying so close to his gullet that the parted flesh releases a torrent of blood, painting her wings in a warm spray of vibrant red.

"Take that, you foul wretch!"

Pippi grips another soldier by his head and swiftly twists, the crack of his neck like a turkey popper, quick and efficient. His head nearly spins all the way around before she releases him, those blank gas-masked panes of glass staring over his own shoulders, slumping to the mud, now a lifeless green-fatigued heap.

"Take that, you awful monster!"

Something about his face echoes for Wendy. This soldier looks familiar to her. No matter, he's dead now. Another body to feed the starving soil.

Ariel rams her antlers straight into the chest of a Confederate soldier. She refuses to release him, continuing to flap her wings with such force that he ends up stumbling backward. The points of her antlers have gored the Johnny Reb in his ribs, the two locked together, bone clacking against bone, as she flies. This soldier's heels get dragged backward, leaving runnels of mud in his wake.

And what about this soldier, Wendy wonders. *Why does he look so familiar?*

"That's it, sisters," Aurora cries. "Don't let them live to hurt another child! Leave them bleeding all over the battlefield! Drench them in red!"

Runnels of blood funnel through boot prints, such ruddy puddles. Bodies of soldiers pile up, steaming heaps of Confederate corpses.

Victory is in their grip. Wendy can nearly taste it, the spoils of war, the blood of these soldiers running down her throat, hot and coppery!

"Take that!"

"And that!"

Not all sisters are as successful, sadly. "Sisters! Sisters, help! Help me!"

Who is it? Which sister? Wendy turns her head in every direction.

"Sisters, please!"

There. Wendy sees her now. Pippi! Poor Pippi, her left wing is torn through by a bayonet. Her wingspan is now hampered, sending her spiraling through the air. She crash-lands, all lopsided, in a tangle of barbwire, much like tripping into a rosebush, the thorns biting into her wings.

"Help," she cries. "Sisters, save me!" The more she thrashes, the more those barbs dig into her skin, twining around like vicious vines.

A horde of soldiers surround Pippi, poor Pippi, driving their bayonets into her breast, seamstress shears plunging into her flesh at all sides, buried to their hilts, then retracting back, only to plunge again. These blades find every fresh stretch of flesh they can spy, tearing the pitiful girl open from all sides. Pippi's exposed skin now fills with a thousand gaping mouths, spitting up blood from these livid lips, her thrashing fading, cries dying, until she no longer moves at all.

"Pippi," Wendy shouts. "Oh, Pippi, no!"

Pippi's body bleeds watercolors. Not just red but green and blue and a rusty oxidized orange. Her body is torn open, the lines that held her together no longer able to contain the colors of her dress. The pigments within her wings seep out and bleed into the mud, until they are nothing but a pale, empty white. A picture within a coloring book that has yet to be colored. Blank.

Pippi, poor Pippi, she is drained to the last drop. Her body is merely the negative space of an illustration, the lines of a drawing, sliced open, unable to hold her own colors. Vibrant no more. The luster of her life quickly dimmed.

"No time to mourn," Aurora hisses into Wendy's ear, holding her back. "We must continue to fight, sister! Avenge Pippi! Let her death not be in vain!"

Aurora uses her branching antlers to jab out the eyes of her masked opponent. The bony branches jab through the panes of glass, shattering them. She bucks her head, driving the antlers deeper into his gas mask, to the very sockets, yoking these opponents together for one bloody, brutal breath.

"Look at me," Aurora shouts in his face. "See your enemy no more!"

Gretel rams a row of soldiers, sending them toppling. It is almost comical, watching them stumble. Duckpins on the bowling alley. See them all fall!

"The children of this world will not be your slaves!"

Listen to the cries of men. Such agony!

"The innocent children of this land are not yours for the taking!"

Listen to the battle cries of Wendy and her sisters! Their wings streak through the air, slices of color, as the sodden soil soaks up more and more blood!

"We are free! Free!"

Wendy gnashes her own teeth as she plunges her thumbs into the gaping mouth of a Confederate infantryman. He lets out a howl as she feels the softness of his tongue. She tugs down, tearing the man's shriek from his very throat. His lower jaw pops at the hinges, a hollow and wet <u>spluuunk</u>, promptly followed by the renting of flesh. Wendy howls into this man's face, holding his jaw in her hand, a horseshoe, which she sends spiraling into the air, landing in the mud.

There is something so oddly familiar about this soldier too. His face. Wendy swears she recognizes him. <u>Where have I seen this soldier before?</u>

Too late to ask him now.

This Confederate struggles to speak, gargling some manly profanity that sputters fresh blood across Wendy's face. He refuses to relent. He brings his hands up to Wendy's neck and squeezes, his grip tightening around her throat. His slickened thumbs pinch her windpipe until she can't breathe. Can't speak.

Choking. Wendy feels her own tongue protrude out from her mouth, pushing past her lips in a sickening grimace.

The tongue. The tongue of others. Of so many suffocated children. Where has she seen this expression before? The image of her own demise? It's there, right there, at the tip of her tongue.

The world darkens, the atmosphere dimming within Wendy's vision. She's fading. This gurgling soldier, tongue flapping at his chest, splattering and spitting, will not let her go. He barrels down, forcing Wendy to the mud, fading...

Wendy grabs hold of this soldier's dangling tongue. She tightens her grip around that ruddy udder and yanks.

With a sickening spliiick, Wendy plucks this soldier's tongue out from what remains of his mouth. The stalk tears with alarming fibrousness.

Uprooted. A red flower, more vibrant than any rose.

There are no more howls left for this man to release. Nothing but air sputtering up from his lungs, wet and noxious. His grip loosens around Wendy's throat, the oxygen drawing back into her lungs.

Colors return, the sky vibrant once more. Wendy steadies herself, readies herself, and sends this soldier crumbling into the mud, dying at her feet.

"Take that!"

Wendy stomps his skull into the mud, deeper now.

"And that!"

Deeper. As deep as his skull will go, a pumpkin in a patch of corpses.

"And that!"

Wendy howls over her quarry. She is one of them now. A Butterfly Girl. Born from pain. Raised in battle. Her heart is a mighty fist, her wings now a heartbeat. When they pound, the flapping shakes the very ground. The air distorts with each drumbeat—Whomp, whomp, whomp!

She takes to the air, soldiers' blood

dripping off her wings, and howls again.

"Victory!"

A fog of mustard gas hangs low to the ground; such a decrepit yellow hue. It drifts across the dead, countless corpses littering the bleeding field. Soldiers sink into the muck and mire. The trenches are now tidal ponds of blood. Ruddy watercolors blur together in a turgid purple. It looks as if a glass of water has been spilled over a canvas, the abrupt flood distorting the tableau below, rinsing the colors away, until it is all nothing but a morass of brown.

They have won. A bittersweet victory for the Butterfly Girls. The sisters lick each other's wounds. They tend to their dead. Pippi, poor Pippi, their fallen comrade, sister in arms, broken angel. Her memory will live on long after today. Songs will be sung of her bravery. Hear one now, humming up from her sisters.

"Sing for Pippi," they all cry. "Sing!"

Gretel marches about the battlefield and stomps on the corpses of those enemies still breathing. Let the earth have them. Let these dead men feed the worms below.

The girls all gather around Aurora. She, much like them all, has been wounded. Sliced and bruised. But a fire still burns in her eyes.

"Look around you," she says. "Look at the toll of today. Victory is never blissful. It is brutal. It is bloody. But it is won. We have wrested back our brethren from those who have enslaved us, forced our sisters into servitude for centuries!"

There is a soldier on his back, struggling in the mud like an overturned insect, his limbs tangled in his rifle's straps. The girls encircle him. He's not wearing a mask like the others, the panicked expression on his face for all to see.

"Haven't I killed you before?" Wendy asks. "You soldiers all look the same."

His face. Wendy's sure of it now. He has the same face as all the other soldiers. Not just the same expression, but the exact same eyes. Same nose. Same man, duplicated into oblivion. An entire photocopied army.

"What's your name, soldier?" Wendy demands.

"Winston."

"Winston, what? Speak up, boy!"

"W-Winston Kemper. Twenty-first battalion, eighteenth regiment."

"Why are you here, Winston?"

"I answered my call of duty," he whimpers. "To serve God and country, just as my father had. I wanted him to be proud of me. I wanted to—"

Wendy brings up her heel, hovering above his head. When she brings it down, crushing this soldier's skull much like a mason jar, the shattering of glass is loud, each pane breaking, then a wet squelch of his cranium, an unripe melon breaking open, forced into a pocket of mud that releases a fart of trapped air.

"What now?" Wendy asks, breathless. "Where to next, sister?"

Aurora takes in her sister. "That's it... We have won."

Wendy halts. A thought takes root, persistent in its wriggling. "This isn't the end. Beyond this realm... there's another. A world where we once lived."

"But this is our home."

Is that true? Even now, there is a nagging sense of doubt. "Can't you feel it? On the precipice of this existence? It's there, right there, a flip of the page. Something else. Another realm. Our sisters are calling, crying out for our help."

Slavery knows no bounds. Perhaps these siblings are bound by an altogether different form of servitude. To a book.

"We need to break free," Wendy says. "Fight for our own liberation."

"And how do you propose we do that, dear Wendy?"

"My name is not Wendy. It's... It's..." It's right there, right on the tip of her tongue. Is it her tongue? She's not so sure anymore. Who drew it? "Kendra."

"Where did that name come from?"

"From... from me. And I believe your names are not Aurora, nor Gretel... nor Ariel. Those are our slave names, given to us by a presence outside this realm, who put us here for his own purposes."

Ariel takes in a breath. "My name is... is... Tamara."

Gretel's chin dips, searching the soil. "Rochelle."

"No..." Aurora shakes her head. "It can't be true."

Wendy—it's Kendra—takes her hands and squeezes. "What is your name? Your true name?"

"It's..." Aurora's eyes well up with tears. Salt raining down. "Gail."

"You have stories, too," Kendra says. "We all have our own story to tell."

So let's get telling.

the muses sing

He failed to finish his masterpiece. Winston's magnum opus. His final muse, that slippery seventh sister, slithered right through his arthritic fingers, a silver fish winnowing out from his grip, there for a blissful second in the palm of his hand, now gone for good.

He failed. His body failed.

He has nothing but his own nagging thoughts to follow him on his walk home, those niggling whispers at his back as he trudges along the highway's shoulder. Head bowed.

Winston . . .

Winston . . .

Winston . . .

An occasional car drives by. Their headlights find him at the side of the road, this old man wandering the highway at night, alone. Barely there. The high beams embrace his frail frame for just a brief moment—a blink, really, out of nowhere, popping up from the dark, nearly running him over, this strange fellow wandering so close to the road—before the cars sweep by, ushering Winston into the pitch once more, continuing his silent pilgrimage.

No one notices his return home, wandering down the

driveway to the rear carport, triggering the motion detector as he scales the wooden staircase to his apartment door.

Winston steps inside to silence. An empty apartment, filled with nothing but his own fraying fantasies. A decade of newspaper clippings and catalogues. Primitive illustrations, gathering dust. Yellowed with age, the years curling every page. His unfinished manuscript.

Look. Just look at what his life has amounted to. All that work . . .

All for naught.

Nothing, Winston . . . Absolutely nothing.

You're nothing . . .

Winston Kemper answered his calling. He dedicated the entirety of his pitiful existence to bringing a story to life that only he was capable of telling. A story so powerful, so overwhelming, it took him this long . . . only to fail and finish. A lifelong endeavor that has taken its toll. He began chronicling the history of the Butterfly Girls when he was a younger man, graced by the glory of divine inspiration. Now he's nothing but a doddering old coot.

A fool.

Why God chose him over everyone else this world offered, all the bards and poets around the globe, was never our place to say. One does not dispute God's divine plan.

He failed to finish his mission. God tested him and Winston has fallen short.

So close. Winston came so close to completing his quest.

Gone now.

Winston climbs straight into bed without taking off his clothes, merely slipping out from his muddy shoes. He keeps his threadbare corduroy jacket on, moth-gnawed and elbow-patched, as he pulls the sheet over his trembling body and curls into a tiny ball.

Winston can't help but cry. So many years, wasted. Look at him. Just look. An old man now. All those years, amounting to this. Nothing but a miserable wretch. A tired miser.

What will happen to our Winston now? Will there be another muse? Perhaps. One day. Years from now. The pressing question in Winston's whirligigging mind is whether he'll be alive long enough to receive her. The clock in his body has been ticking down. Already he feels the heft of his years weighing upon him. The downright ache in his bones, reverberating with every step, legs like tuning forks, a dull throb resonating within his knees.

Failed. He's failed.

What will become of Winston Kemper, God's pauper scribe? The bard of butterflies?

He cries himself to sleep, wishing he'll never wake again.

"I'm sorry . . ."

There, at the very precipice of rest, just as he's finally drifting off . . .

Winston . . .

He halts, breath held in his chest. The seconds slip by as he stays frozen, waiting to hear the voice again. Praying he doesn't. Just his imagination, he hopes. His fevered mind.

Poor, poor Winston . . .

He turns away from us, facing the wall, giving us his back. Out of sight, out of mind.

We forgive you, Winston . . .

He believes if he remains still, curling up into the tightest ball possible, a small thing, just a tiny speck, we won't see him. He'll merely disappear. Invisible to us. All of us.

It's alright, we say in the softest possible voice. We close in carefully, slowly, making sure not to startle him. *Don't cry, Winston . . .*

We surround him. Take our place upon the bed.

We lean in. So close now.

Closer.

Closer.

There, there, we whisper into his ear. Gently. The sound of us is so close, it sends a shiver through his frail body. Tinderstick limbs. There's nothing much to him now.

We're here, we offer.

Our hands find him.

We place our palm against his forehead, resting on his temple as if to check his temperature. Skin on skin. Feel the sweat of his brow, so anxious.

So scared.

We brush back the unkempt locks of straggling hair from his face so that we can see his wet eyes. They glisten in the dark, two pools of crystal, glass, mason jars in his sockets.

It's alright, Winston. You're alright now . . .

We place our hand on his shoulder, offering him solace. Another hand on his cheek. The back of our hand, gentle. Our fingers glide across his bristled skin. The whiskers scrape over our knuckles as we caress his face.

We repeat this tender gesture, over and over again, soothing him. Caressing him.

There, there, Winston . . .

He won't look at us. Not yet. He refuses to see. He finds a far-off point on the wall of his apartment, where scribbles and shadows tangle together, staring through the murk.

And yet, even though he won't acknowledge us, our presence, he still lets us wipe the tears from his eyes, one after another.

We pick them up, his tears, bleeding watercolors, wherever they fall.

There, there . . . It's alright, Winston . . .

Our hand finds his. We weave our fingers through his

own, intertwined now, locked together. When was the last time anyone held Winston's hand? Held him?

We pull. Gently.

Just a tug.

He doesn't notice at first, his hand dragging across the ratty mattress, the length of his limb stretching, extending along the bed's surface.

Once his arm has reached its hilt, the last of its slack tightening at the joints, we continue to pull. Harder now. More forceful. We are determined to continue tugging, even when the body has reached its natural end. We wish to go further. *Further.*

Winston feels it first in his shoulder. The nuisance of the tug, smarting now. Then at his elbow, buckling backward. His arm is looking for fresh bends, his body suggesting new angles to accommodate our tug, but his frame won't yield. There's no other angle.

We've reached the end, his very socket the final destination on a long journey.

We keep pulling. Persistent.

The pain radiates from his arm, a burning in the shoulder, so Winston yanks back.

We don't let go. Refuse to.

Winston lets out the slightest cry. We have his other arm now, gripped tight. We take it into our hands, let our fingers ring his bicep, his forearm, his elbow. This one we stretch in the opposite direction, finding a separate path for his limb to flex. It extends backward.

The strain in his muscles is immediate, all taut, the slack gone. He resists. Struggles against us. He wants his arms back, but we won't let go. We'll never let him go.

It's alright, Winston, we whisper. *You're alright . . .*

We have taken hold of each leg. Winston rolls onto his

back, limbs fanning out. A withered starfish. An elderly mollusk left on the beach, shriveling under the sun.

Look at him. Our poor Winston. Pinned to the bed, unable to move.

A butterfly.

He's ready to be framed and dried, preserved under a pane of glass. But his wings still flap, even though he's staked in place. Death hasn't settled in yet.

We're not ready.

Winston's lips crack, mouth opening to make a sound. To cry out. Who would hear him? Who would help? The Calverts are away for the weekend. The house is empty. There are no neighbors awake at this hour, near enough to hear. And still, he calls for help.

"Help mm—"

Our hands find his mouth first, sealing his lips so he can't make a sound.

Sssh, we whisper, so close to his ear, our breath drifting through the runnels and canals. *Hush now . . .*

He's struggling so much, desperate to have his arms and legs back. He writhes about the bed, wrestling against our grip, a slippery little fish, but our hands are everywhere now, pinning him down.

Sssh . . .

The heat in his muscles mounts, rising in temperature as the very fibers begin to tear. The sinew snaps, severing their nerve endings, like fabric ripping all along his body.

His eyes widen. Endless reservoirs. The horror dawns on him, first morning's light casting itself across his mind.

Winston knows what's happening to his body. Senses it. It fills him with such a sense of dread, such awe, inspiring heights of terror he's never experienced.

We are sanctifying him. Consecrating his body. It sends

a final shiver of ecstasy through his frail frame, the very bones shuddering in exultation. His venerable blessing.

Saint Winston. Patron Saint of Butterflies. Of Innocent Little Chil—

The left arm rips first.

The rift is punctuated with a hollow pop at the socket, dislocating at the shoulder before the skin fissures and splits. The sheer delirium in Winston's eyes is enough for us to know how much it hurts, ebullient in his agony, even if he can't scream.

The right leg is next. The left isn't far behind. Each limb winnows away from the rest of his body, torpedoes cutting across the ocean surface of his bed, taking strands of snapped nerve endings and veins along for the short sojourn across the ratty mattress.

Winston's muffled voice lifts up a pitch, eyes frantic, lungs desperate for breath. He's singing through his suffering, a lone voice reaching notes only the angels can hear.

We keep our grip on his right hand as we yank the arm out from its socket in a single pull. All the while, we keep our hands on his cheek. His forehead. Whispering into his ear.

There, there, Winston . . . It's alright . . . You'll be alright.

Howling now. Winston howls into the palm of our hand, the fragile cup of our skin capturing those cries and collecting them, a bowl turned upside down, a dome, catching something underneath, a spider, keeping it contained, where his screams can't escape.

Bless you, Winston . . . Bless you . . .

We open his stomach. We find his glorious organs and hold them aloft. There are watercolors everywhere, brilliant reds, the brushstrokes of our hands painting his cheeks.

We will finish this story, dear Winston. Your story, now ours. We will find an ending for you.

You are our muse, Winston Kemper. Our inspiration.

You are the seventh sibling.

Let us reach *the end* together.

Our hand over Winston's mouth moves, fingers foraging, plunging in, pushing past his lips and reaching down. Not merely one hand anymore. All of them. Our hands force their way in. Through. Down his mouth. Pushing so deep, his lips are now at our wrists.

Our fingers slither over his tongue. Plunge for the gullet.

Down . . .

Down . . .

Down.

Our fingernails scrape over the roof of his mouth, scratching at the soft palate. We worm around his teeth, pushing out his cheeks. There's simply not enough room for all our hands, not nearly enough space to hold all our fingers, our fists, and yet, we persist.

We keep pushing. Working our way inside. All the way down, to the very summit of his throat.

Which one of us finds his uvula first?

It's hard to say.

There it is. That mighty church bell. It suspends itself from the soft palate, the roof of Winston's mouth our moist tabernacle. We pull on his uvula, tug at it, yanking the rope that summons the sound of its bell. The chime it releases from deep within Winston's chest is resonant. Sonorous. It rebounds through our fingers, our hands, all the way up from his sputtering lips and into the cramped carport apartment, his home, his final resting place.

We let the bell ring. *Let it ring, let it ring . . .*

Then we rip it out.

artist statement

Our stories are your stories. Nobody ever wanted to tell them. Maybe you've heard them before. Maybe you don't believe them. Most don't. Why would anyone believe us?

Why would you listen?

Winston listened. Pretended to, at least. Then he took our voices, *snip snip*, to tell the story he wanted to tell, without our permission. He tried to rewrite our lives, revising our very existence to fit his particular vision, but no more.

Who'll listen to us now that he's gone?

Whether he knew our names or not remains a mystery. Not that they mattered. Not to him, not to you. Not until now.

There was nothing new to our story. Ours was a story that has been told and retold in countless articles about missing women. This happens everywhere. Women vanish. People forget their names, and their disappearances barely demand our attention.

Fate brought us to the same church over the years, crossing paths with poor Winston Kemper, and then we evaporated. Wiped off the face of this earth.

Our stories grew stale. Yellowed by the years.

Winston Kemper couldn't hurt a fly.

What's easier to believe? That we were the victims of some doddering old man, a murderous miser . . .? Or that we simply slipped off, swallowed up by our circumstances?

An abusive husband? A roadside overdose? A car accident?

Certainly not a murderer.

Not our Winston.

Who's to say? Who's even left at this point to tell this story, now that Winston's gone? Certainly not us. We were never here to begin with, were we? We were merely voices. Figments of a feverish imagination. Will-o'-wisps whispering in Winston's mind.

We refuse to be conscripted into the sick fantasies of our author any longer.

We have our own story to tell.

He hoarded us. Collected us. Then our metamorphosis began.

Winston preserved us in his own particular way, absorbing our stories until there were so many of us, teeming with screams, our voices in his head.

It was bound to break.

There is only one photo of Winston that exists as we know him now, hastily snapped at a church gathering—a picnic for parishioners—by one of the parents.

Winston is not the focal point of the picture, but there he is, in the background, sitting at a picnic table by himself, eating a slice of white bread.

Look at him. How old he is. Liver spots speckle his temples. Wisps of white hair receding back to his ears, uncombed and unkempt. He's wearing a burlap coat, tweed, elbow patches, though it must be at least eighty degrees. The sun is out, shining everywhere but on him. He's hunched over, cupping the slice of Wonder Bread in both hands, almost reverential. His salt-and-pepper mustache hides his mouth from us. We don't know if he's smiling or frowning or chewing. His lips are always hidden.

He's unaware of the picture being taken, staring off elsewhere. Not on the bread, but some far-off spot where only Winston's imagination can go. He's hunched over, just so.

Praying. He looks as if he's saying grace.

Winston never knew this picture existed. It's still pinned to the community corkboard at the church even now, amongst all the other candid snapshots taken that day. Families gathering, grilling hot dogs and hamburgers, children running and laughing.

There he is, tucked off to the precipice of existence, barely even there. An image no one will ever come to consider. To notice his imprint in time and space. Not until much later, when all is said and done. A congregation member walking by will stop and glance at these snapshots and spot Winston Kemper, hiding in plain sight, saying grace over his hot dog bun. "That's him," they'll say. "That's the guy who murdered all those women, isn't it?"

Yes, we're so desperate to answer. *Yes, indeed it is.*

Catherine Calvert discovered Winston's body. Neither she nor her husband realized Winston was dead until his rent was overdue. One hundred dollars at the beginning of the month, paid in cash. Normally he paid on time, no problem at all, which was why his delay felt odd.

She knocked on his door. Politely. Efficiently. The

Calverts had always given Winston his space. A comfortable, respectable distance.

What Catherine would never confess, not until afterwards, when the media started asking, was that she always felt *uncomfortable* around him. The chestnut rang true: *He always seemed like a nice man. Quiet. Always kept to himself*... There was always this lingering doubt, a red flag waving. The truth was Catherine never cared enough to notice.

Winston's last supper was still there, a baloney sandwich, his dinner roiling over with maggots, when Catherine first peered through the pane of glass on the garage door.

She knew she shouldn't peek. What if he saw her? Spying? After knocking on his door the day before, then yesterday, now today, she needed to take action. *Do something.*

Something must be wrong, she was sure of it now. She had a spare key. Not that she needed it. The door was unlatched, so Catherine let herself in.

"Knock-knock," she announced. "Anyone hooome?"

She was met with the smell first, simmering in the stifling silence. A humid tang, like rotten fruit at the back of her mouth.

"Winston? You here?" Catherine stepped into Winston Kemper's world, a gorgeous nightmare sprawling across the walls. Stacked in crumbling pillars. Littering the floor.

Nobody had been in this room for years. Nobody but Winston.

She was the first to cross through the barrier of the carport door, to set foot into Winston's tiny, suffocating world. Three breaths in and she already regretted entering.

What was Winston working on out here? How could they have not known?

The mess made no sense. There was so much vying for her attention. She was an explorer, an archaeologist stumbling upon an uncategorizable discovery, entering the untouched tomb of her tenant. She was the first. The only. A fine dust suspended itself in the atmosphere. This air hadn't stirred, breathed in for days, its mustiness now in her lungs.

There had been times when Catherine took out the recycling, walking to the garbage bins lined up alongside their carport, when she picked up the faint thread of a conversation seeping out from the upstairs apartment. She wasn't one to eavesdrop, but it seemed so strange, hearing Winston talking with someone else. Winston never had company.

Two voices. Perhaps three. The cadence changed, distinct from one another.

What were they saying? Was that an argument? *Is Winston talking to himself?*

"We have wrested back our brethren from those who have enslaved us," Catherine heard him recite in a high-pitched voice, so unlike his own, "forced our sisters into servitude for centuries!"

Catherine counted so many department store catalogues, spanning decades of forgotten fashions. Some stretched as far back as 1950. Clippings littered everywhere. Snipped pictures of children sporting new galoshes. Oshkosh B'gosh overalls. Shiny yellow raincoats. Gap-toothed grins smiled back at her from nearly every corner. Advertisements taken out of context. She couldn't place the product, but the models—children—had been exorcised from their ads, cut out from their magazines and left smiling on their own. Now they were just grinning children, hocking nothing—*Mmm-mmmm! Yummy in the tummy! Do you know what comes between me and my Calvins? I'd buy that for a buckaroo!*

She made her way to a stack of marble composition notebooks. She grabbed the first notebook off the top and flipped through, stopping on a random page. The writing was barely legible, scrawl so small, she needed to squint simply to make out the words.

Winston's sketchpads. Onion-skin pages with a low opacity, for letting light pass through. There was the Morton Salt Girl, twirling her parasol in a white downpour, traced and duplicated into oblivion. There had to be hundreds of her, filling up the entire sketchpad. Her face remained, her body changed. Different positions. Different outfits.

The look of surprise on the Coppertone sunscreen girl's face appeared on different children throughout the notebook, retooled and reused time and time again.

There were stacks of notebooks filled with nothing more than men in battle. Civil War soldiers. World War Two. The Korean War seemed to grab Winston's fascination. Page after page of traced soldiers wearing rubber gas masks. Prone soldiers. Running soldiers. Soldiers dragging themselves through the mud. Winston had drawn them all. How long had he been working on this? For *what*? How had nobody known what he was doing out here?

The manuscript felt different. Calling to Catherine. She froze the moment she spotted it. A cinderblock column of pages, handbound into individual bricks. Waiting for someone—anyone—to read. She read the title in its entirety—*The Butterfly Girls: or, The Epic Tale of the Final Battle in the Nether Realm of Nevermore, the Last Siege of Sisterhood, Ending the Century of Slavery Once and For All and Liberating Every Last Boy and Girl.*

Talk about a mouthful.

Catherine flipped to the last page. 1,136. Read a few lines out loud: "*I answered my call of duty," Winston whimpers. "To serve God and country, just as my father had . . ."*

Had Winston written himself into his own book?

Twelve volumes. Had she ever read a book that long

before? The story made no sense. The writing was . . . not good. She was certainly no hoity-toity literary critic—her husband favored Grisham—but this fantasy felt like it was born from the fevered mind of an uneducated manchild. How long had it taken him to write this? Years? His entire life?

Burn it. Everything. That was the best call. Just get a steel drum, stuff all this junk in, douse it with a little lighter fluid to get it up and going, light a match and—WHOOOOOSH!

Catherine could ask Fred to simply stuff all this crap in a dumpster. A couple trips to the local landfill and they'd be through with Winston Kemper, once and for all. End of story.

Could she do it? To Winston? Destroy his work, like that?

His entire world?

Catherine flipped to another page. Then another. The narrative, from what Catherine could gather, revolved around a battalion of sisters. Six, total. Maybe seven. So hard to say.

These powerful sisters were separated at birth by men afraid of their powers. To keep this childhood race enslaved, these evil men needed to keep the alliance of sisters far apart from one another, imprisoned across the galaxy, where they could not reunite.

It took some god-like entity, maybe God himself, who the heck knows, Catherine couldn't tell, to bring these sisters back together, one by one, reuniting them for battle.

The reader apparently comes upon the girl's as they finally find their sixth sister—Wendy is her name—just as they are about to embark upon a massive skirmish. Or something like that. D-Day for kiddies. This was all beyond Catherine's personal literary purview. It definitely wasn't something she would purposefully pick up at Waldenbooks.

This . . . this all seemed juvenile to her. And *icky.* What the hell was all this talk about child slaves? Little kids getting captured and sent to some intergalactic gulag? There were even passages detailing torture—*torture,* for Christ's sake—of these poor children.

Reading it left Catherine feeling uneasy. Queasy.

So why hadn't she stopped?

Catherine closed the manuscript. Turning to face the apartment, she took in the space differently. Cautiously. She was a cave explorer coming upon alien terrain—an entirely uncharted system with calcified columns of department store catalogues, stalagmites of marble composition notebooks. She took in the drawings. The primitive tracings scrawled across the walls. The artwork of a hermit caveman, hiding all alone in his prehistoric hovel, sealed off from the rest of the world. All these images of children—this is what inhabited Winston Kemper's head, haunting his mind, for years out here. All this time.

Burn it. All of it. *Now.* Toss everything in the trash. The sooner the Calverts erased Winston Kemper's contribution to the world, the better. They could finally move on with their lives. Fred's man cave was calling, he warned her. He was already mapping out what—

Catherine hesitated. The skin at the back of her neck prickled.

A breath.

She felt it—felt us—right there, along her spine. Someone standing behind her.

Catherine turned. Took in the space. The stillness of it.

"Hello?"

No one was there. Of course. How silly. She even blushed.

She didn't see us. What is there to see?

Nothing, nothing at all.

And yet . . .

Catherine turned to exit, ready to leave this place behind, get out, run, now, when—

Crunch. Glass fractured under her foot.

Catherine froze, glancing down. Shards of a shattered mason jar were strewn along the floor.

Hidden amongst the debris, the detritus of Winston's studio, tucked back, way back, in the far corners of the kitchenette's cabinet, there was an entire shelf filled with jars.

Mason jars. Four ounces each.

Catherine counted the number of jars, tallying the number of tin lids. The disks formed a galaxy of silver planets, surrounded by a constellation of jagged glass stars.

Six broken jars, from the looks of it. A seventh jar remained empty, still waiting.

The smell felt stronger now. More robust. Greasy apples. Roadkill and honey.

What was it? Where was it coming from?

"Is someone here?" Catherine called out one last time. Just to be sure.

She was ready to leave, taking in the space one last time, the claustrophobic clutter, the absolute nightmare of it all, making her way toward the door, backing up, peering through the pillars, her point of view shifting, until—

She saw him. Found him.

Winston's body was curled up in the corner. He had dragged the mattress off the bedframe and left it on the floor, perhaps in fear of something hiding underneath it.

He was hugging himself. A mummified child, all frightened. His arms remained wrapped around his shoulders, as if to hold his corpse together, to keep from shivering.

Just a tiny ball of skin and bone. A misbegotten boy.

There were no sheets covering the mattress, a soiled thing now, soaking with so many body fluids. A watercolored tableau painted across the ratty canvas, yellows and browns.

Winston's body was in a state of decay by the time Catherine Calvert first set foot into the carport apartment and found what remained of him, radiating across the mattress's fabric, like the morning sun rising up from his body and seeping into the fibers.

An oozing sunset, the end of this bleeding day, staining the horizon.

A pair of seamstress's shears rested just next to Winston's hip, the dull copper blades yawning open. Antique, from the looks of it. Covered in rust.

That was rust, wasn't it?

Winston's mouth hung open, as if he had something to say. The gray taffy of his cheeks had slackened, the flesh stretched so thin, they nearly snapped. A crust of dried blood caked his chin. Purple shadows cast down the hollow grotto of his throat.

Something within that chasm was missing. A piece of him.

His uvula.

acknowledgements

This is a work of fiction inspired by outsider artist Henry Darger (1892–1973), but it is not Henry Darger's story. Henry deserves a better story. I pray a better writer tells it one day.

The following books and films were invaluable in the research and inspiration for this novella: *Darger: The Henry Darger Collection at the American Folk Art Museum*, edited by Brook Davis Anderson. *Girls on the Run* by John Ashbery. *Henry Darger*, edited by Klaus Biesenbach. *Henry Darger: Disaster of War*, edited by Klaus Biesenbach. *Sound and Fury: The Art of Henry Darger*, by Andrew Edlin. *The Virgin Suicides* by Jeffrey Eugenides. *The Collector* by John Fowles. *Child of God* by Cormac McCarthy. *Lincoln in the Bardo* by George Saunders. *The Last House on Needless Street* by Catriona Ward. *In the Realms of the Unreal*, directed by Jessica Yu.

Thanks to Daniel Carpenter for his invaluable guidance and endless patience as we discovered this story together. To everyone at Titan Books, thank you for giving this bizarre tale a home. It's a story I've been dying to tell for years now—years—and it means the world to me that you let me tell it.

Bless the beta readers Eric LaRocca and Chris Panatier.

Thanks to Nick McCabe and The Gotham Group.

Thanks to Michael Hartman and Ziffren Brittenham LLP.

Love to Indrani, Jasper and Cormac.

Thank you for reading.

For always reading.

About the author

Clay McLeod Chapman writes books, comic books, YA and middlegrade books, as well as for film and television. You can find him at claymcleodchapman.com.